Almon Trask Allis

Uncle Alvin at home and abroad

Almon Trask Allis

Uncle Alvin at home and abroad

ISBN/EAN: 9783743376205

Manufactured in Europe, USA, Canada, Australia, Japa

Cover: Foto ©Andreas Hilbeck / pixelio.de

Manufactured and distributed by brebook publishing software (www.brebook.com)

Almon Trask Allis

Uncle Alvin at home and abroad

ALMON TRASK ALLIS.

Uncle Alvin

Home and Abroad

BY

ALMON TRASK ALLIS

PUBLISHED FOR THE AUTHOR
1895

DEDICATION.

To every patriot, who loves his country better than his party ; to every mother, who loves her home and children better than all else but her honor ; to every christian, who loves the kingdom of Jesus Christ better than his own indolent ease ; to every member of the world's W. C. T. U., who are struggling so nobly and against such unequal odds for the uplifting of their own sex, not only, but are rendering such signal service to the cause of moral reform throughout the world, is this little volume most respectfully dedicated.

PREFACE.

I SEND forth this child of my musing with something the feeling which I imagine a parent must feel when the son or daughter leaves the roof-tree to make their way in the world for themselves, knowing little what reception the world will accord it.

Yet I think I feel less solicitude concerning it than a parent would for their child, under like circumstance ; and, for this reason, if the world turn coldly upon it, neither this offspring nor myself will suffer by it.

I have written the greater portion of this volume under the pressure of strong conviction.   As long as the conditions remain which called out these utterances, so long will these voices ring, even if the world does not hear.   If they shall accomplish little in the way of bringing about a better condition of things, they will at least register my unqualified protest.   I send them forth without apology.

The fact that many of them seem to have a somewhat local importance and application can hardly be charged as an element for criticism ; for, while that is true, it is also true that there can scarcely be found a large town or city where similar or worse conditions do not exist.   What seems, therefore, to be local needs only a slight effort of imagination to transfer the field into any other place, to be as applicable and pertinent as if written from that standpoint.

I do not do as most authors are doing with their maiden literary efforts, crave the indulgence of the public ; I do not even crave that of my critics : the one thing I ask is fairness.

Neither do I appeal for the co-operation of my friends. The cause of humanity and religion and good government are broader and higher than mere individual interests ; and if this work can contribute, in any sense, to either, I shall feel amply compensated ; but mere personal favors are not to be considered. Those who believe as I believe, and feel as I feel, will need no other incentive than that which has actuated me in writing, to further the circulation of this little work, for the sake of what it aims to do, just in proportion as they think its circulation will minister to that end.

The writer believes that there is patriotism enough in this nation, and virtue enough in the citizenship, when it is once aroused, to strike down with relentless hands the perils which threaten ; but he also believes that our greatest perils are from our moral inertia, our fancied security in the presence of real danger. Just how to arouse the thought and patriotism of the masses, or what shall be the agency by which it shall be done, is quite another thing.

What I have here written has not been written in any spirit of bitterness or egotism, but I have tried to do some real uncovering. And it can hardly be that any reader shall follow me through this little volume without a tolerably fair understanding of things as I see them. That others shall see them with my eyes I hardly expect. Yet it will rarely occur that one can read this volume from start to finish and not receive some of the spirit which has been so manifestly the "inspiration" of the author's work.

I wish here to publicly acknowledge my lasting obligation to many of my fellow citizens for their generous faith in this enterprise, by giving their subscriptions for the work before it was sent to the printer, thus helping to make the venture possible, as it otherwise would not have been, certainly not until a later date. My sincere hope is that all such shall not find the finished work which they have helped to forward a disappointment.

I have used plain speech : I see no occasion for any other. Mincing matters of public morals brings forth no fruit. False modesty, which dares not call things by their real names, has no part in a moral reform. People who are so fastidious as to be shocked by the reading of plain truths may live to be worse shocked by having the steel of relentless facts enter their own souls. Possibly such may turn away from perusing these lines ; if so, it is well. My messages are to earnest souls, who live to help their fellow men, though it must needs take them into unpleasant conditions, and face even repulsive facts.

There is never a sensation of pleasure in a sur-

geon's probe, but his usefulness would be greatly
hindered without it, and the life of many a patient
might pay the forfeit of his lack.   So the probing of
moral deep-seated abscesses are anything but agree-
able, but who does not see the necessity?

Shutting our eyes to any conditions does not prove
that those conditions do not exist ; it rather proves
our blindness or imbecility.   No man is so much a
coward as he who refuses to look existing things
squarely in the face.   And so I send forth this little
volume with the faith that the intelligent public will,
at least, approve its object.

I may say, incidentally, that I have sufficient material already on hand for a second volume, but
whether it shall ever appear will depend on the reception accorded this.

Respectfully,
ALMON TRASK ALLIS.

Hornellsville, N. Y.

CONTENTS.

UNCLE ALVIN
AT HOME AND ABROAD.

TIT-FOR-TAT.

We read the party papers, each of which will fix the
    blame
Upon the other fellows, and will tell us how it came,
That out of great prosperity there came this sudden
    drop,
And things are takin' such a slide we wonder where
    they'll stop.
One lays it all to Sherman, and the bullion he has
    bought;
The other says the tariff scare the dreadful work has
    wrought;
And so the two old parties are engaged in quite a spat,
Which seems about as dignified as children's tit-for-tat.

The nation's representatives in extra session sit,
And talk about the panic, and the thing that causes it,
With just about the wisdom of the common party press,
And act about as earnest to relieve the great distress.

They spend two weeks discussin', simply lettin' off
    their wind,
Without an expectation that they'll change somebody's
    mind;
Till those who read the papers most must wonder what
    they're at,
Which gives it dignity above a game of tit-for-tat.

That we are in a "pickle" there is no one left to doubt,
But what has got us in it, or the way to get us out,
Seems Greek to all our statesmen, by the way they
    hesitate,
And do so much discussin' there before they legislate;
And one of two conclusions must be forced on every
    mind,
That they don't know the causes, nor a remedy can
    find,
Or, if they know a remedy, prefer to sit and spat,
Rather than to apply it, and to spoil the game they're
    at.   •

One thing is very evident: we lose a lot of "scum"
From our commercial kettle when these boilin' panics
    come;
And when the great convulsion spews it all outside
    the rim,
The commerce of the country settles down in better
    trim.
But what produced the boilin', or what generates the
    "scum,"

Affords the politicians a most palatable crumb,
About which they can wrangle, in the game which
      they are at,
Of wallopin' each other in their pleasant tit-for-tat.

And when our people's habits shall adjust the flow of
      bile,
So they will not be bilious, or have fevers for a while,
Their mental apprehension may at length become so
      clear
That they can tell the causes for this present bilious
      year;
And when at length they find them—if indeed they
      ever do—
They'll find them to be somethin' else than rates of
      revenue,
Or buyin' silver bullion—as they're chargin' in their
      spat—
First one and then the other, in this game of tit-for-tat.

The people's modes of livin', and of business—in the
      past—
Has been a sort of diet that is bearin' fruit at last;
About as vicious eatin', or one's practices defile
The fluids of the body, and will make the fountains vile;
And nature—wiser than we all—will set herself about
The nasty yet important task of vomitin' it out.
The process must be painful, yet must come, for all
      of that,
Or death and putrefaction will begin their tit-for-tat.

And governments are much the same. The politicians
        play
With things of gravest interest, while we jog on our
        way,
And let them do our thinkin', and are easily cajoled
To follow them as leaders, by believin' what we're
        told;
Till sometime we are wakened by a sudden crash, to
        find—
Like others we have read about—the "blind have led
        the blind."
And all are "ditched" together; when we all resume
        our spat
About what caused the tumble, in a rousin' tit-for-tat.

Yet one thing is apparent; there's an over-rulin' eye
Which scans the very thoughts of men, from where
        He sits on high,
And makes their human blindness, in some measure,
        to fulfill,
Without their even knowin' it, the purpose of His will.
And what we call calamity is often just the thing
He hitches on His chariot wheels prosperity to bring;
And does it quite as often while the politicians spat,
And charge the gravest follies on each other tit-for-tat.

THE NEW SOPRANO.

We always thought that singin', in the service of the
    Lord,
Was just as much a worship as the preachin' of the
    word ;
And often we've been lifted, by some good old-
    fashioned hymn,
To almost scale the jasper walls, and get a glimpse of
    Him ;
For, somehow, with the melody a stealin' through my
    soul,
I've seemed to stand above the place where "waves of
    trouble roll,"
And felt within my bosom, what can hardly be ex-
    pressed,
The tides of glory surgin' in "across my peaceful
    breast."

We never knew just what was meant about a "cul-
    tured ear,"
But thought that songs, as well as prayers, were for
    the Lord to hear;
And if the singer didn't always strike a perfect chord,
It might be worship, just the same, and "singin' to
    the Lord."
And since I've been converted it has ever been my aim
To use what little voice I had to praise His blessed
    name,

By takin' part in prayer and song, and do the best I
  could,
Because at least the language of my heart was understood.

And since they got the organ, and an organist to play,
It kind o' keeps a person's voice from goin' much
  astray;
And I could join more heartily, and not have any fear
Of slidin' up or down too far, and jar somebody's ear.
The choir was no objection, while the good old hymns
  were sung,
Or new ones voicin' worship for the human heart and
  tongue.
Indeed, I rather liked it, for they kind o' went ahead,
So those who couldn't sing by note might follow where
  they led.

But somethin' struck our chorister as quite the proper
  thing,
To get a new soprano—one they had to pay to sing—
Because her voice and ''culture'' had superiority
Above the persons who were glad to give their service
  free.
I didn't know about it, and the services began,
Without a deviation from the customary plan;—
The openin' hymn was read and sung; the pastor
  knelt in prayer,
And everything betokened there was worship every-
  where.

But when the prayer was ended, and the people raised
    their eyes,
They saw the new soprano, in the organ loft, arise,
And wondered what was comin', but they didn't won-
    der long,
For she began to warble what they called a sacred
    song.
We don't know why they named it so, because it rose
    and fell,
From tones of soft contralto to a veritable yell;
And though we gave the best of heed our two ears
    could command,
"Good tidings" was the only thing that we could
    understand.

'Twas somethin' like a whirlwind, which will often
    start in low,
And then shoot up, and up, and up, to see how high
    't can go.
It might be sacred music, but it didn't well compare
With what it followed after—such a tender, searchin'
    prayer!
It didn't help devotion, when the people had to strain
To catch what she was sayin', and then find it was in
    vain.
It might as well been Latin to the most of those who
    heard,
Because the best of ears could catch but now and then
    a word.

Aud when I asked about her, I was greatly shocked
　　to hear
That she gives dancin' lessons for a portion of the year,
And there she was a leadin' us—or singin' in our
　　place—
To bear the worship of our hearts up to the throne of
　　grace.
And then I wondered if the Lord would be well pleased
　　to hear
The voice of such a medium between us and his ear,
And if a cultured voice, like her's, was more of a de-
　　light
To Him than simpler worship, where his people could
　　unite?

I don't know but I'm fogyish, but I can't make it
　　seem
That tunes are really sacred, where the singer has to
　　scream;
Or that the folks are edified, who, havin' ears to
　　hear,
Can get but now and then a word that falls upon their
　　ear.
And I can't fully understand why one who has been
　　blest
With vocal powers of extra grade should sing for all
　　the rest,
While they must sit and listen to a string of vocal
　　noise,
Suggestin' more of operas than of celestial joys.

And I am so old-fashioned as to think, and dare to say,
That singin' isn't worship, when they're doin' it for
pay.
'Twill do for entertainments; but it's quite another
thing
To do it in an audience before the Heavenly King.
He listens more for heart-throbs than for choicest
"runs" or "trills,"
And nothin' discords in His ears where love the music
thrills.
If we can sing by proxy—as so many think we may—
It must be as acceptable to do it when we pray.

If one is only "gifted"—as some people truly are—
Why shouldn't such an one be hired to lead in public
prayer?
He needn't be a christian, any more to pray than sing,
If we can hire somebody else to do our worshiping.
We don't suppose the Lord objects to any kind of art
Which doesn't come to intercept the worship of the
heart;
But who believes a moment that the terrible "I Am"
Can look with slightest favor upon any sort of sham?

We needn't wonder very much that converts are so
scarce,
Where "art" has made the worship little better than a
farce.
We'd like to see things comin' back to good old-
fashioned ways,

When congregations all were joined in songs of hearty
        praise;—
When pulpits and the pews were moved with only one
        desire,
To be baptized together with the Holy Ghost and fire;—
When simple-hearted faith could grasp the promise of
        the word,
And bring a speedy answer from the presence of the
        Lord.

We'd like to see our services a good deal more devout,
With all of these "performances" for worldly ears left
        out,
And everything like "merchandise" completely swept
        away
From every form of worship, on the holy Sabbath day.
We don't know as we'll see it, but we hope it won't be
        long,
Before the church will cease to pay a singer for a song,
But out of hearts—renewed by grace—the anthems
        shall arise,
Fillin' His earthly courts with praise, and reachin' to
        the skies.

PAT. RAGANS' REPLY.

'Twas on election mornin', in the Spring of ninety-one,
When fever heat was gettin' high with candidates that
 run,
And all their "heelers" were alert to work each doubt-
 ful man
In favor of their candidates, as only "heelers" can;
For then, besides the interests which always enter in
To such a local struggle where each party hopes to
 win,
The "local option" issue let each freeman's ballot say,
Without regard to party, whether drink should go or
 stay.

Pat was a good mechanic, and commanded, at his
 trade,
About the highest wages which the wagon makers paid,
And might have kept his family with every need sup-
 plied,
And have a margin over for the luxuries beside;
Or been the owner of a home, instead of paying rent,
If all the wages he had earned could have been wisely
 spent.
But somehow, though he learned a trade, he never
 learned to think,
And so—like many other men—his wages went for
 drink.

'Twas no uncommon thing for him, when he had
      drawn his pay,
Before he reached his wretched home to "blow" it all
      away;
And then the shifts that he must make to tide him
      through the week
Subtracted from his manhood as it added to his cheek,
And made his credit worthless, and his patronage a
      bore,
And him, or any one he sent, unwelcome at the
      store,
And made his wife and children hear his footsteps
      with a dread,
And sent them often shivering and supperless to bed.

But somehow, for a day or two, some light had struck
      his brain;
A single thought had taken root, and things were get-
      tin' plain.
He saw how foolish he had been to work from day to
      day
And furnish some one else's home with what he drew
      for pay,
While those whom he had sworn to love, and who
      looked up to him,
And had the right to do it, had been farin' mighty
      slim;
And he had registered a vow as solemn as he knew,
That after this, "*Pat Ragan might be counted on as
      true.*"

He hadn't reasoned rapidly, but when the truth was
    clear,
It swept through all his Irish soul, and trembled in a
    tear,
And took the form of high resolve that never once
    again
Should Patrick Ragan's hat sit on a whisky muddled
    brain,
And that on this election day—the first time in his
    life—
He'd cast his Irish ballot for his babies and his wife,
And send the "cussed" traffic, which had proven such
    a foe,
As far as he could send it, where it's author was—be-
    low.

Just then the shop door opened, and a step and face he
    knew,
With all the old time confidence, came briskly walkin'
    through,
And after shakin' hands with Pat, in his familiar way,
Said, "Well, my man, I s'pose you know that this is
    'lection day,
And we expect that all the boys will help us in this
    fight,
To score another victory for freedom by to-night.
I'll tell you Pat, those fellows who would take your
    rights away,
Are gatherin' their forces, and will hit us hard to-day.

"But Pat, my boy, I know your heart, that you are al-
       ways true,
And we who stand for liberty can always count on
       you."
Pat listened quite respectfully to what the fellow said,
And then his hand went slowly up to his uncovered
       head,
And ran his bony fingers through his mass of curly
       hair,
As if he felt for somethin' that was shyly hidin' there,
And then, as if he'd found it and had somehow let it
       slip,
The thought that he had loosened he had caught upon
       his lip—

"No, Mr. Murphy," answered Pat, "whativer ye ex-
       pect,
The mon that ye are talkin' for, me vote won't help
       elect."
"Why, Patrick Ragan," Murphy said, in such un-
       feigned surprise
That one could almost hung his hat upon the fellow's
       eyes,
"What on the earth has happened?   Have you lost
       your head to-day,
And do you really mean that you shall vote the other
       way?"
"As true as preachin'," answered Pat, "That's just
       the thing I mane,
I'll niver vote for license in this livin' world again."

"But, Pat," began the "heeler," "don't you know
    that if you beat,
You'll kill the business so that grass will grow in
    every street?"
"Be gorrah, then," was Pat's reply, "I'll git meself a
    cow,
And feed her on the common in the summer anyhow,
And Biddy and the babies shall have somethin' more
    to eat
Than they've been used to havin' if the grass grows
    in the street.
I only hope it's comin' in the way that ye avow,
For what I'll save from drinkin' grog will soon give
    us the cow."

"I've been a fool, as ye well know, and let you fellows
    lead,
And voted as ye told me while me family were in
    need;
I've voted for the drink-shops, and gone in their open
    door,
To waste me hard-earned wages, and have kept me
    family poor,
While those who got me money for the rot-gut that
    they sold,
Had silk to dress their daughters with, and jewelry of
    gold,
With feather beds to sleep upon, and with fine up-
    holstered chairs,
And carpets spread on every room, includin' hall and
    stairs.

"While me poor wife and babies are ashamed to walk
    the street,
Because they're dressed so poorly by the side of those
    they meet;
And don't have any company to visit them at home,
Because me house is furnished so that no one cares to
    come;
And when they see their finery me money helps to buy,
Do you suppose its weakness that compels me wife to
    cry ?
And when she knows me money keeps these families
    well fed,
Does that make her less hungry goin' supperless to
    bed ?

"I've always voted license, as ye told me to, before,
But hain't the liberty you've prached just kept me
    family poor,
And me a drunkard, so that when I rached me home
    at night,
I've met me patient wife with blows, and killed me
    babes with fright ?
The liberty ye promise is a blarsted lie and cheat,
And, by the powers above me, I will tread it under
    feet.
I don't know how it happened, but the divil—by
    misthake—
Must got a trifle slapy, for he let me git awake.

"And since me eyes are open, and me fetters have
    been broke,
Do ye suppose Pat Ragan will be puttin' on the yoke
That's made a baste of him these years, and wasted all
    his pay,
And beggared those who loved him, in a most in-
    human way;
And all to plase the people, like your honor, who pre-
    tend
To be so anxious for me rights because ye are me
    friend?
Excuse me, Mr. Murphy, but me eyes are open now,
And I will take me chances with the grass and with
    the cow."

DEDICATION OF A CHURCH ORGAN.

*A Gift From a Member of the Congregation, Costing
$1,000.*

We thank Thee, Oh, Lord, for this gracious display
Of Providence standing before us to-day.
Thou sawest, from Heaven, our recognized need,
And filled it, at length, by this generous deed.
However concealed from the donor it be,
The impulse to do it was given by Thee.
No purpose to render Thy church on the earth
Such aid could have other than heavenly birth.

3

We thank Thee, at length, that Thy kingdom of grace
Hath found, in this heart, such a sure lodging place:—
That up from the seed Thou hast sown in the past,
Thus much of a harvest has risen at last:—
It may not be much for Thine eyes to behold
A steward returning a share of Thy gold,
Which out of Thy treasury freely hast lent,
To bring—at Thine asking—the owner's per cent.

But surely the seed of Thy kingdom has brought
Some fruit, by inspiring this generous thought,
Which gave us the beautiful organ we play,
To blend in the worship we offer to-day.
Grant now, and henceforth, as the weeks come and go,
Thy kingdom—thus planted—may flourish and grow,
Till from this beginning Thou soon mayest see,
Himself—as an offering—given to Thee.

And spare him the folly—most graciously spare—
Of spurning the gift Thou hast gone to prepare,
Of glory and honor forever on high,
And choosing thy mercy and love to defy.
But give such a voice to the music which floats,
From Sabbath to Sabbath, from each of these notes,
That oft as he hears them, each minor and chord,
Shall speak to his heart, as the voice of the Lord.

Let blessing and mercy accompany song,
Inspiring the weak, and directing the strong;
Let truths of salvation which fall from the tongue
Reach hearts, to uplift them; though spoken or sung,

Let music be clothed with the breath of Thy power,
For comfort or courage, in sunshine or shower;
Let freshness and beauty, like dewdrops, distill,
To brighten and strengthen for doing Thy will.

And grant that this offering made to Thee here
May voice our thanksgiving for many a year;
And echo and echo the message of grace
To those who come after, from this sacred place.
Forbid, we implore thee, our Father, forbid,
Thy purpose of mercy should ever be hid
In formal devotion, to simulate praise,
And blend in the music which this organ plays.

But make it to be, even more than we dare
To hope or to ask, in the words of our prayer,
A blessing which pastor and people shall see
Potential for winning the wayward to Thee.
To Thee—aye, to Thee—while the privilege waits,
And beckons and beckons them into her gates,
With grateful assurance again and again,
That none ever seek for admission in vain.

UNCLE ALVIN ON THE SITUATION.

The fact that these are stirrin' times is tolerably clear,
And also that the stirrin' is increasin' year by year;
But just what is the cause of it, or what it signifies,
Is just about as clear as mud in most of people's eyes.
Some say it's lack of money, that is causin' such un-
        rest,
By which the whole republic is so frequently dis-
        tressed,
Because of commerce throttled, and of business standin'
        still,
Awaitin' some decision of a single person's will.
And some will tell us gravely, that the cause of this
        unrest
Is all because the workin' man is grievously oppressed,
In both the hours of labor that shall constitute a day,
And in the compensation which is given him, as pay.
While all the politicians—or the most of them, at
        least—
Will tell us that the tariff should be lessened, or in-
        creased;
And that upon this issue all the burdens must be laid,
Which causes this uneasiness, with labor, and in trade.
The moralists and preachers (the majority, I think),
And mothers of the nation, see the trouble in the
        drink.

That there is trouble somewhere here, and of the
      gravest kind,
Is clear enough—as it would seem—to stir the dullest
      mind;
Yet, somehow, our humanity is made up so perverse,
That evils which are recognized can grow from bad
      to worse,
'Till they become a mighty leech, whose suckin' lips
      can drain
The life and strength of nations; yet they let the thing
      remain.
What makes the minds of men so dull we need not
      here discuss,
But can not well ignore it, with the facts confrontin' us.
Results must have their causes; and all fruit suggests
      a tree;
And so there must be somethin' back of all the wrongs
      we see.
And if we go a huntin', with a view to find the cause,
We'll find it back of governments, and back of all the
      laws;
For governments are nothin' but the people's will ex-
      pressed,
And law is but the fingers that is doin' all the rest.
If government is vicious, or the laws are workin'
      wrong,
And people feel dissatisfied, they needn't stand it long,
For they can re-construct it, and compel it to fulfill,
In all important interests, the sovereign people's will.
The trouble lies about in this:—while wrongs may be
      increased,

The *ones* who *feel their burdens worst,* are those who
    think the *least,*
And deem it patriotic, if they sort of go it blind,
By followin' some leaders with a battered axe to grind.
One needn't go to college, and become a graduate,
To know a little somethin' of the runnin' of the State;
For if he looks about him, there's enough for him to
    see,
To educate him fairly, what a citizen should be,
And what his rights amount to, and if he shall be op-
    pressed,
About what course he should pursue, to have his
    wrongs redressed.
The *trouble lies* in *thinkin'*—for they never learned
    the trade—
But mostly get opinions, like their breeches, ready-
    made,
And let the politicians, who will guarantee a fit
As good as tailors, get the stuff and see to makin' it;
And some will stay the corners with a sort of extra
    strip,
To keep the seams from baggin', and prevent an awk-
    ward rip;
And then, of course, they wear it, and will join in the
    parade,
And look as nice as "dummies" in the suits these fel-
    lows made,
And represent about as much of other people's
    brains,
But count as much as livin' men in forgin' their own
    chains.

About how much, for pity's sake, need any person
    think,
Before it's clear as daylight, what he ought to do
    with drink ?
They needn't know the figures that record the many
    slain,
Who might be livin', but for it, throughout our wide
    domain;
And needn't count the money which is squandered
    every year,
Because this mighty spendthrift is allowed to tarry
    here;
And needn't hear the sobbin' of the broken-hearted
    wives,
A countless army of them, weepin' over blighted lives;
And needn't see the children, which it dresses so in
    rags,
Or women, who, from angels, it develops into hags;
And needn't see the prisons which it does so much to
    fill,
Or figure up the taxes for the prosecutin' bill;
And needn't see the mothers, who are cryin' for their
    boys—
An awful army of them—which it every year destroys;
And needn't count the fortunes by the drinkin' busi-
    ness sunk,
But only *need* the *knowledge* that the *drinkin' makes*
    men drunk.
Ye God ! is that as nothin', which destroys a fellow's
    brain,

And makes a mind irrational, and fires up every vein,
And cooks the nervous substances, and puts men on
        the rack,
And takes the manhood out of him, but never brings
        it back?
A little thing—a trifle, to be puttin' on a yoke,
Which seldom, in the later years, is put aside or broke?
A habit to be trifled with, which generates more pain,
And fills more hearts with agony, and counts more
        victims slain,
And spreads more desolation on the bosom of the earth
Than all the epidemics since creation had its birth?
And yet to-day the nations have all taken an affright
About the spread of cholera (and well, indeed, they
        might),
And every paper everywhere is spreadin' the alarm,
And every government on earth is stretchin' out its arm
To build up such defenses as they can against this foe,
Or drive it from their borders by the quickest way
        they know.
And this is well, and argues much, when such an
        estimate
Is placed upon the lives of men, by nations small and
        great ;
And every effort of them all should have a warm
        "God speed,"
As well as what assistance, in the way of help, they
        need.
But doesn't it look mighty strange, that after all they
        say,

And all they do, to keep or drive this fearful plague
    away,
That every one of them have got—and seem content
    to keep—
A scourge more terrible than this—with more relent-
    less sweep—
And one which festers rottenness and death on every
    air,
And spreads its vile contagion through the nations
    everywhere,
And strikes down man and womanhood of every rank
    and age,
And all of them protect it, both by law and patronage?
The awful scourge of cholera has something in its tread
Which fills the minds of men with awe, and strikes
    their hearts with dread ;
Its march is so imperious that where it plants its feet
All but the most intrepid ones are swift in their retreat.
Its conquest over human lives is less by its own might
Than by the subtle power it has of killin' men by
    fright.
Yet one thing can be said of it—in sort of doubtful
    praise—
It gathers in its harvest fast, and quits : it never stays.
It swings its scythe so rapidly that people, when they
    fall,
Lose but their lives ; not virtue, fortune, honor, all :
Men die as men, and leave a name unsullied by its
    touch ;
Their bodies, not their characters, have felt its awful
    clutch ;

Posterity has something left to which their love may
     cling,
And weave a chaplet for the name, to make the mem-
     ory sing.
It comes to nations suddenly, as by a mighty leap
From out its unknown caverns, where so many mys-
     teries sleep,
And pounces down unheralded, and thrusts its sickle in
Whenever and wherever it chooses to begin.
But though its chariot wheels of death are driven with
     such speed,
The spirit which possesses it is not insatiate greed ;
But rather, as God's scavenger, wherever it is seen,
It comes as Heaven's board of health, to keep the
     nations clean,
And stirs up human common sense to move itself about,
And wash and dig, and scrub and dust, and get the
     garbage out ;
And then it hies itself away, and lies down in its lair,
Until the scourge of human filth invites it back some-
     where.
And to the credit of our race (a shameful compliment),
This scourge of human nastiness is somewhat rarely
     sent ;
Yet, if my memory hasn't slipped, the worst it ever did
In any of its visits here would be completely hid,
Comparin' ghastly records with it, any single year
Of any generation, by the scourge we harbor here :
And everybody frightened so, seems little less than
     "rot,"

About the scourge of cholera, while huggin' what
      they've got.
I'm not a politician—and I thank the Lord I'm not—
And so am left more free to use what little sense I've
      got ;
And if it's good for anything, the workin's of my
      mind
Have this one virtue, that they're not of an expensive
      kind ;
But all the world is welcome to whatever I may think,
And what my reason teaches me we'd better do with
      drink.
It certainly is good or bad.   If good, it ought to stay;
If bad, what baby doesn't know it should be put away ?
And what's the verdict of the world, but that it is the
      worst
Of all the many evils by which men were ever cursed ?
Bad ! bad ! and only bad ! possessin' not a single trait
Which, without great distortion, can its evils mitigate.
And yet, in a republic where each voter is a king,.
The people don't know what to do with this accursed
      thing !
They snivel at the dreadful crimes and wrongs it per-
      petrates,
But give it license to remain in almost all our States :
Nay, more, they give it sanction, and protect it from
      its foes,
By laws as strong as government, as he who fights it
      knows.
Oh, men of free America, what stultifies you so,
That you can't see how to be rid of this relentless foe ?

It's just as clear as broad daylight, to those with half
       an eye,
That freemen can be rid of it if earnestly they try.
Stop snivelin' at its awful deeds, and deal it such a
       blow,
With every ballot that you cast, that it can't help but
       go.
It got intrenched by freemen's votes behind its barri-
       cade,
And hisses its defiance from the breastworks we have
       made.
If ballots built its breastworks, cannot ballots tear
       away,
And leave it unprotected, for its enemies to slay?
Either acknowledge we are serfs, and alcohol our king,
Or smite it with the fist of law and slay the hateful
       thing.
There's only this conclusion, if we let the thing remain,
We countenance its evils for the purposes of gain ;
Or else we fear to strike, as a serf to strike his king ;
Or we prefer to have it stay, because we love the thing.

UNCLE ALVIN AND THE STREET CARS.

Well ! I have seen the street cars run, the fust I ever
saw,
With nothin' anywhere in sight that looked like it
could draw;
And yet the pesky things will pull (or push) a mortal
load,
And stop and start as easy like as horses on the road,
And go as fast, it seemed to me, as most o' horses run,
And nothin' round to sweat or foam—it really looked
like fun;
And then no driver's hollerin'; no clatterin' horses feet;
No wearin' out the pavement in the middle of the
street.

But I confess I couldn't see how anything so wild
As what we call 'lectricity could ever come so mild
And gentle like, as if at last it more than half en-
joyed
Wearin' a sort o' harness, and a bein' thus employed.
But, my ! I thought that after all it's mighty slippery
stuff,
And if it got a tantrum, when they'd worked it long
enough,
That like as not 'twould jump the wires, and hit some-
body's head,
And, quicker'n you could wink your eye, the feller
would be dead.

It seems to me it's ticklish like, to be a settin' there,
With lightnin' all around you and a runnin' every-
     where;
A comin' down from overhead, and passin' through
     the seat,
(Or somewhere—don't exactly know) or underneath
     your feet;
And all the while it's workin' so there's nothin' to be
     seen,
And nothin' heard, except the groan of workin' the
     machine;
But then it's there, and there in force, as any one may
     know,
For if it wasn't, then of course, the cars they wouldn't
     go.

I seen so many people ride the fust day I was there,
I almost thought I'd try it too, but didn't hardly dare,
For somethin' kept a whisperin', "I guess you'd
     better wait;
I guess, perhaps, they'll stay awhile, and it won't be
     too late,
And if the lightnin' jumps the wires, and hits some-
     body's head,
If you ain't there, it won't be you, but some one else
     instead."
So I looked on, and peeked around, and watched them
     as they run,
And got some knowledge, anyway, if others got the
     fun.

And if the lightnin', all the while, shall prove itself
    as tame,
And always act as civilized as it has since they came,
The cars will prove a blessin' to the ones who love to
    ride,
(If nickles don't give out) and pay the management
    beside;
And next time I'm in town and think that I've a coin
    to spare
(And like as not that time won't be until the comin'
    fair),
I think I'll take a ride or two to see how it will seem
To ride along the city streets with lightnin' for a team.

UNCLE ALVIN COMES TO THE FAIR.

I'd been a-thinkin' all along of goin' to the fair,
And promised Nancy Jane we'd try the street cars
    while we're there ;
But thought the third day, like enough, would be
    about the best,
For we enjoy the seein' of a crowd, with all the rest ;
For, somehow, I have noticed if the crowd is kept
    away,
A fair is called a failure, with the best of a display,
But never knew exactly why it should be reckoned so,
Unless it takes the quarters of the crowd to make it go.

So Wednesday mornin' early we got up and flew
    around
(For when it comes to hurryin' we ain't quite run
    aground,
If we are not as suple, 'cause our limbs are growin'
    old,
And half my hair has gone away, and hers has lost its
    gold),
And had our chores all done up nice, and breakfast
    put away,
By six o'clock, and started out to have our holiday,
The first we'd either of us had in quite a lengthy
    spell,
And meant to have a good one if we both of us kept
    well.

And when the horse was put away, and I had seen
    him fed,
And waited 'til the hostler run the carriage in the
    shed,
We started for the fair ; but when the street cars came
    along,
Both cars were full already to the steps, with such a
    throng !
The seats were full, the aisles were filled as full as
    they could stand,
And hung along up over head, a-holdin' by the hand ;
And so I said to Nancy that we'd have to wait awhile,
And then if we don't get a ride you'll see your uncle
    smile.

"You see," I said to Nancy, "that on any such a day
The cars will be 'most empty when they go the other
    way,
And we can ride them down and back for just another
    dime,
And have our choice of seats, besides, and reach the
    fair in time."
And so we waited where we stood, and 'twasn't long
    to wait,
Until the train came pullin' back at quite a lively gait,
And stopped for us to get aboard, for I suppose they
    knew,
Some way or other, just about what we had planned
    to do.

Then how they ran! just slackin' up in makin' of the
    curves,
And lettin' people off, sometimes, to kind o' help our
    nerves;
Till, most before we knew it, they were slackin' up
    their pace,
And in about a minute they had reached their stoppin'
    place.
I wondered how they'd start them back, and I got off
    to see,
And saw them swing the trolley pole—'twas done so
    easily—
And saw a thing in either end, some smaller than a
    churn,
And on the top a little crank the driver has to turn.

4

And so it's all the same to them which end shall go
    ahead,
Because the car has two machines, so the conductor
    said.
But goin' back, I must confess, that, gray-haired as I
    am,
I don't remember ever bein' caught in such a jam.
They stopped at every crossin', and at lots of times
    between,
And such a scramble to get on I'm sure I'd never seen;
And long before we reached the fair, the idea one
    would form
Would be about two hives of bees the night before
    they swarm.

Once, after they had stopped, I guess the driver
    turned the crank
And let the current on too quick ; it gave us such a
    yank
It almost took us off our seats, and made the ladies
    scream,
And made me think 'lectricity a rather fractious team,
That needed for a driver one who understood the bit,
And all about the tacklin' that is used in workin' it,
Or he is liable to have, if not a runaway,
At least a lively fracas, and to have it any day.

And I confess my wonder grew, the more of it I saw,
And don't know where the limit is of what this team
    will draw ;

For when they loaded these two cars with five-and-
        twenty ton,
It didn't make them hard to start, or change the speed
        they run.
And all the while of goin' up I sat and racked my
        brain
To try and make it comprehend what power ran the
        train,
But only got as far as this : it's part of Nature's plan
That all her mighty forces should be workin' so for
        man.

And all of them, I notice, in the things they do for us,
Perform their work so quietly, without a bit of fuss,
That if we didn't see results we would almost declare
That there was nothin' goin' on, in Nature, anywhere;
While all the time her great machine is runnin' on so
        still,
And turnin' out the things we need, like grists from
        out a mill.
But suddenly the cars were stopped before the fair
        ground gate,
And everybody walked away with his or her own
        freight.

UNCLE ALVIN INSIDE THE FAIR.

I noticed some who came with us who didn't have to
        wait
To buy themselves a ticket, but they pointed for the
        gate,
While we, who hadn't got them, had to push ourselves
        along,
As fast as we could do it, through the jostle of the
        throng,
Till we could reach the window; then we had awhile
        to wait,
Because they, couldn't serve us, for the crowdin' was
        so great;
And when we got them, we were hustled through a
        clothes-reel gate,
Which clicked, to register, I suppose, at quite a lively
        rate.
And when, at last, we found ourselves fairly within
        the ground,
We had to stop a little bit, to sort o' look around,
And calculate, as best we could, which way we'd
        better go,
With somethin' like a system, so we'd take in all the
        show.
But we decided that we wouldn't hurry through,
As most of those who come with us seemed eagerly
        to do;

And so we loitered leisurely, and got in folks's way,
And stopped in front of every place to take in the display.
'Twas rather nice, the most of it, but what we'd seen before,
And lots of times, when we had been a shoppin' at the store.
About the only difference, when all is said and done,
Between the stores and bein' here, here's several in one.
One thing I've often noticed, and I saw the same thing there,
That character will show itself, and almost anywhere ;
The breadth, or scanty pattern, after which men have been made,
Without their even knowin' it, is sure to be displayed.
For instance: here's a music man, that occupies one side,
And just across the ten foot hall, the space is occupied
By Business College people, doin' samples of their work,
And givin' advertisements, through the fingers of a clerk;
And he, the music dealer, shuts out all the light behind,
By hangin' up some curtains, and by closin' every blind,
That all the light that comes to him might come across the way,
And strike his instruments in front, thus helpin' his display;

While they, the College people, who are on the other
      side,
Are by this little act of his compelled to open wide,
And work in their own shadows, but it's all the same
      to me,
Only such narrow spots in men I seldom fail to see.
The thing which interested me as much, and I think
      more
Than all the rest together, that was on the bottom
      floor,
Was just a lot of dishes that was shown us by a man,
Himself and all his trinkets, that had come from old
      Japan.
I watched him open boxes and undo the chunks of
      straw,
Put up the most ingeniously of things I ever saw,
And not a piece of chinaware had lost a little chip,
Though comin' such a distance, both by railroad and
      by ship.
The vases, pitchers, urns and things I didn't know
      the name,
And never saw the like of them before these dishes
      came,
With tiny cups and saucers that were large enough to
      hold
An ordinary swallow (if the liquid should be cold,
And one was not compelled to taste and drink by
      little sips,
Because the beverage was hot and burned his mouth
      and lips),
And little spoons for holdin' pins, and little crocodiles,

That looked to be good natured—for their mouths
    were wreathed in smiles;
And many things beside them, as the advertisers say,
"Too numerous to mention," in at least a half a day.
And I suppose the questions that were asked this
    Japanese
Were just to hear his answers, for he tried so hard to
    please,
And spoke our language fairly, so that one could
    understand,
Yet with an accent that betrayed what was his father-
    land.
And yet he did some business; for some people stopped
    to buy
These trinkets which had come so far, through curi-
    osity,
As I suppose, that somehow, in the presence of such
    things,
Their thoughts could take a journey, and their fancy
    stretch her wings
To where the dusky fingers had so curiously wrought,
Into a shape so beautiful, some humble pagan's
    thought.
Another thing we noticed was a pyramid of bread,
Piled up in one exhibit—of two wagon loads, they said,
And which the women had brought in, contestin' for
    a prize,
That seemed to have, with lots of them, a dazzle for
    their eyes;
Some dealer offered a gold watch to anyone who made

The choicest loaf of home-made bread, from flour of
    certain grade;
And here was what had come of it; what sacks of flour
    they sold,
And how the eager women tried, attracted by the gold,
For, somehow, such a prize as that will move a
    woman's breast
About as much as 'twill a man's, to do their level best.
And so about two hundred of them eagerly went in
To such a hurdle race as this, where only one could
    win.
And then I went to wonderin' about how much is made
By dealers who resort to such a doubtful trick of trade.
Of course, it adds a little spice, and makes a little fun,
But does it prove a benefit to trade, in the long run?
Don't it most always happen, that contestin' women
    know
That somethin' wasn't fair about decisions rendered so?
And when the thing is over, don't a lot of them feel
    sour,
And ready to declare that all the fault was in the flour?
In fact, I heard them talkin', in a doubtful sort of way,
About this very brand of flour, and heard one of them
    say,
That it was good for certain things, but that she didn't
    find
The qualities they needed in a brand of flour combined.
Don't such excitin' contests often prove to be unjust,
And often do a quite a lot toward breedin' of distrust?
And ain't it rather vicious, to be temptin', with a prize,
A person into buyin' what they won't do otherwise?

And yet we see it practiced in most every kind of trade,
By offers so invitin', by the way which they are made,
That, really, one would almost think, if words mean
    anything,
That they were rich and generous, with fortunes there
    to fling
To almost any kind of chap that had a mind to take
The slice which they would give him, in the offer
    which they make.
But I suppose there's somethin' in the way which men
    are made,
That forms a sort of reason for their makin' this parade;
I don't know what to call it, but it's in them just the
    same,
And works them as effectually as though it had a name,
A somethin' that is ready to be stretchin' out the hand
To pick up any offer which they do not understand,
If only there is in it but a chance for them to make
A dollar's worth of profit for a penny's worth of stake.
And if they see against them, as a hundred is to one—
A sight for bein' punished for the chances which they
    run,
Yet if the offer made them has a smack of value in it,
They'll take the single chance they see, a hopin' they
    may win it.
And it don't count a feather's weight about the ninety-
    nine
Who took the other chances, and are hold of the same
    line,
To know that everyone must lose, if they should
    chance to win,

While they who swing the pot for both will rake their
      shekels in.

But men are much like fish who bite most any kind of
      bait,

If it is kept a movin', and like them, repent too late,

And don't get much the wiser for their havin' bitten
      once,

But when another bait is flung, again they play the
      dunce.

Up stairs we found a lot of things that Nancy liked to
      see,

But hadn't much of interest to persons such as me,

And so I spent a quite a while and followed her
      around—

For there, a person could get lost much easier than
      found—

And looked at pictures, bric-a-brac, and things which
      they call art,

So long I thought that Nancy would have learned
      them all by heart ;

And it was long past dinner time before we found a
      seat,

And left off lookin' long enough to take a bite to eat.

And then, when we felt rested, we set out to see the
      stock,

And found that they had gathered quite a large and
      handsome flock,

And most of them were awful fat, especially the sheep,

And many cattle, and some hogs—too fat, I thought,
      to keep;

For if it's profit that they want, it don't pay very well

To keep an animal in stock when fat enough to sell.
But while we went from pen to pen, the bells began
    to ring,
And people crowded toward the park, and set us won-
    dering
What it could mean, and why the crowd were pushin'
    over there
With such apparent haste, as if they had no time to
    spare,
And might be late for somethin' which they wanted
    so to see,
That pretty soon it somewhat roused our curiosity ;
And we joined in the tide of folks without our knowin'
    why,
Except the feelin' that we had to sort o' gratify.
But 'twasn't long we had to wait before the thing was
    plain,
And, bein' we were in the crowd, we thought we
    might remain,
And listen to the music that was comin' from the band,
And see what entertainment there was just about at
    hand.
And so, before we knew it, men and women climbed
    the fence,
And craned their necks and trembled in a kind o'
    vague suspense ;
And down the track where they were lookin', sure
    enough, we saw
The contest that was comin', and possessed such pow-
    er to draw ;

For, side by side, the track was filled with half a dozen
    steed,
With each a jockey driver, for a trial of their speed ;
And everybody in the crowd, almost, it seemed to me,
Had caught the spirit of the race, and watched it
    narrowly ;
And when a horse, no matter which, struck out a
    neck ahead,
They'd stake their money on him, whether well or
    poorly bred,
For pedigree don't count for much, and registered or
    not,
In such excitin' times as this, but whether he can trot ;
It's simply speed and bottom, though ungainly as a cow,
Which makes the horse a favorite, and takes the
    money now.
It isn't what he looks to be, in graceful form or limb,
Or in the "style" he may put on, that gives the race
    to him ;
Nobody seems to care to-day especially for show,
But every one is cheerin' on the horses that can go.
And when the race was finished it was captured by a
    nag
That half the crowd, before they started, called a
    "scalawag."
And while they gave the winner such a volume of
    applause,
I couldn't keep from thinkin' it was one of Heaven's
    laws
That's not so much in promise, of the many who begin,
But in the pertinacity and energy to win,

That gives the race to any one, of high or lowly birth,
And in the end will take him for about what he is
    worth.
One thing seemed strange about this fair : it came to
    me that day
With somethin' like a thunderbolt, while viewin' this
    display :
They call it agricultural, to help the farmers show
The products of their industry, in anything they grow,
And offer manufacturers inducements every year
To bring whatever they produce, for exhibition here ;
And ask of everybody else, with somethin' fine to
    show,
To bring it here, where people come, to let the people
    know.
But when I saw the programme, and the offers that
    are made,
And saw the size of premiums on articles displayed,
And noticed how the races and the other things com-
    pare,
It seemed to me they gave the "trot" more than the
    lion's share.
And then I followed down the list, as careful as I could,
To see if farmers owned the nags that trotted here so
    good,
But not a solitary horse, as near as I could find,
That figured in the races here, of any sort or kind,
Belonged to any farmer of the country, far or near ;
But they were "horses of the turf," that were attract-
    ed here

By premiums and purses which our "farmers" ad-
          vertise,
So out of all proportion in the matter of their size.
And then the thought came stealin' in, like the gray
          streaks of dawn
Into the blackness of the night, until its shades are
          gone,
That all this "fair" is gotten up (though they will
          swear it's not)
To gather in a lot of folks to see their yearly "trot."
And while I thought about it, and had read the pro-
          gramme through,
I saw the devil's cloven foot protrudin' into view,
And saw how cleverly he'd wooled the christian peo-
          ple's eyes,
Till they believed, and helped along, one of his art-
          ful lies ;
For many of "The Farmers' Club" are christian
          men, in name,
And count as such before the world—above reproach
          or blame ;
Yet, somehow, he has roped them in, and got them
          in the net
His crafty mind concocted and his wily fingers set,
And made them actors in a scheme—because they do
          it best—
Which, if the mask were torn away, they'd every one
          detest.
I thought these christian farmers hadn't many of them
          read,

To any great advantage, what the gracious Lord has
    said,
Of "bein' wise as serpents while as harmless as a
    dove,"
Or of their "tryin' spirits, so that they might clearly
    prove
What sort of spirit they are of," before they lend their
    name
To any scheme which might retard the cause for
    which He came.
I fancied, too, that I could see how broadly he would
    grin
While lookin' at the workin' of his scheme to rope
    them in ;
And almost heard his chuckle, softly fallin' on my ear,
Because of "christian fellowship" which he gets,
    year by year,
From easy goin' consciences, which let him have his
    way,
And plan the sort of pleasures that shall form their
    holiday.
And so the best thing he could do was plannin' such
    a plot
To get a lot of christian men to have a yearly "trot,"
And advertise it widely, and to make it all the worse,
Hold out a bribe for scamps to come, by offerin' a purse.
The "sports" of almost all the States are sure to find
    the place,
When bills and daily papers widely advertise the race.
And here we have the sequence ; for the gamblers
    have the game

To which they've been invited, and are richer for the
     same ;
And when it's off they may retire with profits they
     have made,
And leave these christian gentlemen to see the bills
     are paid :
And since he finds it works so well he tries it every-
     where,
And makes the race the drawing card of almost every
     fair ;
And christian men and women help to make the year-
     ly race
By placin' their exhibits there—a most attractive
     place :
And then their namin' it a "fair" is just the sugar-
     plum
Which lures the better class of folks to spend a day,
     and come,
And get themselves excited as they look upon the
     "heat,"
Where patient animals are lashed for all they're worth,
     to beat.
I wondered, while I witnessed it, if any one but me
Could see in such a contest nothin' else but cruelty.
Six men were drivin' horses 'til their carcasses were
     wet,
And every nerve and fibre were as tense as could be
     set ;
With eyes a-lookin' wildly, and their bellows pumpin'
     fast

To keep the breath within them, as they all went flyin'
      past ;
And all for our amusement—and the sweepin' of the
      stake,
Which meant, for them that got it, quite a handsome
      sum to make.
We truly must be christians (with a vengeance) if we
      find
That givin' pain to animals brings pleasure to our
      mind ;
And yet there's somethin' in it, or the people wouldn't
      go
And spend their time and money, too, to witness such
      a show.
I went away a thinkin', in a somewhat solemn vein,
About how fast the gospel will extend it's bright do-
      main,
'Til all the world is bathed in light, and hails the
      Prince of Peace
As their acknowledged King and Lord, and sin and
      wrong shall cease,
If those who represent Him here can find some good
      excuse
To put away integrity just for a Sunday's use;
But otherwise are just the same as those who occupy
An attitude which sets them down His open enemy.
Oh, weak-kneed christianity! you need to grow some
      bone,
Or wear a plaster on your back, 'til you shall dare to
      own,

In face of men or devils, that you've no apology
To make to anybody, as excuse for loyalty.
You need to learn the lesson which His enemies can
    teach,
In all their daily doin's, and the manner of their
    speech ;
For they don't go a wearin' such a look upon their
    face
That makes one think them conscious of their bein'
    out of place ;
And they don't—by their manner—act as if they were
    afraid,
The course of life which they pursue would injure them
    in trade,
Or cost them valued friendships, or in any way de-
    tract
From their supreme advantage, by the way they talk
    or act;
But they are so out-spoken as to leave no one in doubt,
And give no false impressions in their business life, or
    out,
Concernin' where to find them on the questions of the
    day,
And ask nobody's pardon for the things they do or say.
But christians are so cowardly, it isn't much surprise
That those who only know the Lord, through them,
    almost despise
His gospel, as they see it lived by people everywhere,
And count themselves about as good remainin' as they
    are.

We started from the races in a quizzin' frame of mind,
To see what other sort of things we possibly might
     find;
And came—without our lookin'—where the people
     acted queer
When callin' for their "nectar," which was nothin'
     else but beer ;
And we remembered havin' read, on bills they sent
     around,
That nothin that intoxicates would be upon the
     ground;
And here were men a sellin' it to everyone 'twould
     buy,
Where anyone could see them who possessed a half an
     eye;
And then we wondered more and more if christian
     men could sell
The "privilege" these fellows had, then turn around
     and tell
The public—through the papers—that no liquors
     would be sold,
And have the people undeceived, before their lie was
     cold.
And farther on was music, that was comin' from a hall,
And when we got up closer, we could hear somebody
     call
The changes of a dance within, and through the open
     door
Could see the dancers promenade across the dancin'
     floor;

And right beside the entrance was a person that we
    knew
A-dealin out a beverage that wasn't "honey dew,"
But looked a sight like lager beer, to all the thirsty
    men —
For women don't get dry for beer, exceptin' now and
    then.
And here the "cheat" appeared again, as plain as
    anywhere,
That's practiced by the people who had gotten up the
    fair :
They'd said, in all the papers, that 'twould be a moral
    show,
To which the most refined of folks would find it nice
    to go;
And men could take their families, to spend a holiday,
Without their seein' things to make them wish they'd
    stayed away.
And just as we were startin' home—before we left the
    ground—
We saw a fellow carryin' a lettered banner round,
Sayin' on every side of it, that entrance would be free
All night, to those who wished to dance, or those who
    wished to see.
And we began to wonder more about this "moral
    show,"
While thinkin' what a pretty place 'twould be for girls
    to go:
And what a heightened moral treat this dance afforded
    those

Who hanker for such pleasure, if their parents don't
    oppose.
The gates are open all night long, to take in all that
    come,
Alike from virtue's cultured home, or from the lowest
    slum,
And none to challenge any's right to be in any set,
Provided he will pay, with any " partner " he can get:
And who don't know the characters that flock to such
    a place ?
And who can share their pleasures without sharin'
    their disgrace?
And yet the managers of this reputed moral show,
Become a party, by consent, to things so base and low
That no reputed journalist would dare to print the
    name,
And even hints of it would tinge a modest cheek with
    shame.
And I went home a thinkin', but I haven't solved it
    yet,
How long the church of God must wait before its
    members get
That common sense that's sanctified enough to not
    consent
To every plan of Satan to extend his government,
By that old stale device of his, " the nickle in the slot,"
For which they seemed so willin' to endorse a
    " dance " or " trot,"
Under the worst conditions for the fosterin' of truth,
But best for the corruptin' of the virtue of our youth.

I don't know as the most of fairs are planned, and
    mostly run,
On such a "free and easy" scale as people found this
    one;
But I have my suspicions—though of course, I do not
    know—
That few of them are models, as a place for folks to go.
A fair, itself, is good enough, if nothin but a fair,
And may be made attractive by the people's bringin'
    there,
Not only fruits of nature, but the handiwork of art,
Enough to spur the laggin' mind, and educate the
    heart,
And have it free from every scheme of doubtful ten-
    dency,
And good enough for parents and their families to see.
But when the managers of fairs adroitly sandwich in
The beer, and trot, and smutty dance, to lure folks on
    to sin,
It looks to me as if 'twas time for christians to pro-
    test,
And do at least as much as this : refuse to be their
    guest;
For if they haven't "vim" enough, to make their
    protest heard,
I'm sure that they can make it felt, and needn't say a
    word.
The absence of their "quarter," and their absence
    from the crowd,
Would give their protest quite a voice, and make it
    pretty loud;

So loud, that if repeated with persistence, year by
      year,
The managers—though stupid—would be very apt to
      hear ;
And hear where they are sensitive, in an emphatic way,
Because, without a patronage, the fairs would fail to
      pay.
Let public sentiment compel exhibits to be clean,
Which ask for public patronage, by lettin' it be seen
That nothin' else is tolerated ; then, and not before,
These "smutty" exhibitions will be offered them no
      more.

UNCLE ALVIN TO THE BOYS.

Say, boys, I'd like to tell you, if you'll let me have
      your ear—
Now you are gettin' old enough—some things you
      ought to hear.
It may be you have noticed, if you've given it a
      thought,
How boys begin a habit without ever bein' taught.
It doesn't matter any what the habit is to be,
You start it just to follow some example that you see.
For instance : when a fellow that is bigger, some,
      than you,
Is doin' almost anything he hadn't ought to do,
There's somethin' in your bosom that at once begins
      the plea
That you can do the very same, and just as well as he ;

And so, to prove it to yourself, at once begin to try,
And practice it as often as you can, upon the sly ;
And bye and bye, as you succeed—no matter what it
    be—
You feel a little pride, at last, in lettin' others see.
At first, you gather up the "stubs" which men have
    thrown away,
And beg a match, and have a smoke, as often as you
    may ;
And when you get a nickel which you dare to spend,
    you go
And buy a box of cigarettes, and then you have a
    show.
Again, you're in the company of men and boys some-
    where,
And in their conversation you will sometimes hear
    them swear ;
And you will think it manly just to talk as others do,
And use the same expressions, and will soon be
    swearin', too.
And like as not there's some of you who possibly may
    think
'Twill help to make a man of you if you can learn to
    drink ;
But, boys, I want to tell you that it's better to be
    clean,
And let your lips be pure and sweet, no matter what
    you've seen.
If people who are older haven't sense enough to think´
That whisky and tobacco are not good to chew and
    drink,

Why, then you'd better show them, by the contrast
    there will be
Between themselves and those who keep from such a
    habit free.
You set it down as certain that with whisky in your
    skin
Your manhood has gone out as fast as whisky has
    come in.
The two don't dwell together, for they never can abide
The presence of each other long in any human hide :
The manhood will assert itself and dominate the soul,
Or whisky burn the manhood out and have the full
    control.
And, boys, to think that human lips which never
    breathe a prayer,
Or thank the Lord for anything, should ever curse and
    swear ;
And if you think it manly, boys, to do a thing so
    mean,
There must be somethin' wrong about your reckonin'
    machine :   .
I'll tell you 'tisn't manly, but it's everything that's
    low
For either boys or men to treat the Lord Almighty so.
You do a little thinkin', boys, and don't you imitate
The sins of anybody else—however small or great.
You'll grow to manhood faster, and will be a better
    man,
To keep yourselves as far away from vices as you can.
Another thing you ought to know—I guess, perhaps
    you do—

That all the world's best places wait for those who're
    always true.
It looks, sometimes, I will admit, like fightin' with
    your fate,
To have the world ag'in you, in the way they operate ;
But truth, my boy, is mightier, and does more for a
    man,
And gives a boy a higher boost than ever falsehoods
    can.
You try it, boys, and keep your lips unsullied by a lie,
And you'll see how 'twill help you in life's struggles,
    bye and bye.
And there's another thing, my boys, it gives me pain
    to see,
And makes the one who does it seem as mean as mean
    can be ;
And that is makin' anyone a butt of ridicule;
No matter where it happens, on the streets, or at the
    school—
Either because they haven't got the nicest kind of
    clothes,
Or, possibly, don't know as much as t'other fellow
    knows.
You may have seen them do it, boys, or if you ever do,
Just ask yourself how you would feel if that poor boy
    was you ?
Of course, there's lots of boobies, who are big enough
    for men,
Who haven't got the common sense of boys of eight
    or ten ;

Who seem to take a pleasure in tormentin' persons so,
Who don't know quite as much, perhaps, as these boys
     think they know :
But boobies wearin' whiskers often give themselves
     away,
Like donkeys wearin' horses' hides, as often as they
     bray.
Don't you become a booby, boys, and don't you ridi-
     cule
A person dressed in shabby clothes, a cripple or a fool.
If you can wear a better suit than they, you may be
     glad,
But wearin' seedy clothes, my boy, is never half as
     bad
As bein' mean to anyone, no matter what they do,
Or whether they don't know as much or dress as well
     as you.
It's their misfortune if they don't, and they are not
     to blame,
And if they were, your mockin' them would be an
     act of shame.
You'd better be a manly boy, however large or small,
And show that you have self-respect, by bein' kind
     to all.
And then, my boys, you'll find this world a busy place
     to live,
And some one has to gather all the honey for the hive.
The things which give you comfort, both to eat and
     drink and wear,
Don't gather of their own accord, without somebody's
     care ;

It takes a lot of thinkin', and a lot of work beside,
To gather up the things you need and have your
    wants supplied ;
And you can't be expected, as a manly boy, to shirk
The burdens that must fall on you in such a world of
    work :
So don't you get a notion that you'll take it easy long,
Or wear your muscles out in play when you get big
    and strong ;
But jerk your jackets off, my boys, and be a little man,
By doin' any honest work the very best you can.
Let fools and dudes stick up their nose because your
    hands are black,
But, boys, if you have self-respect you'll never snivel
    back,
But jog along as unconcerned as though they wasn't·
    there,
For those who sneer at honest work are no good any-
    where.
And then, my boys, if I were you, because so much
    depends,
I think I'd take a look ahead and see how this life
    ends ;
Because, you know, there'll come a time—and you
    don't know how quick—
When you won't feel like work or play, because
    you're very sick ;
And when some undertaker 'll hang some crape upon
    the door,
And people passin' by the house will say "he is no
    more."

And tenderly some lovin' hands will take your lifeless
    clay,
And in a little narrow house will bury it away.
But, boys, there's somethin' after that, for livin' here
    below
Is not the only stoppin' place that you and I shall
    know :
There's somethin' said about a place, in some old book
    I've read,
Where people have a consciousness after the body's
    dead ;
And if it's so—as we believe—we cannot well afford
To set aside the counsel and the wishes of the Lord.
And so I'd study that old book a little every day,
Which tells about that other life, and points us out
    the way :
And I am satisfied He knows just what His people
    need,
And how to get them safe to heaven, if they will let
    him lead.
And is it strange to you, my boys, if people disobey
The counsel He has given them, that they should lose
    the way,
And when they reach the crossin' they should ascer-
    tain, too late,
The way which they had traveled didn't reach the
    "pearly gate ?"
Would you be disappointed much to find you'd missed
    the place
Which you supposed awaited you, provided by His
    grace,

And found, instead of golden streets and crowns of
    victory,
That "outer darkness" was your lot for all eternity?
I think there's somethin' said somewhere, if I have
    read it right,
That those who don't obey His word are banished
    from His sight :
And how could He be Lord at all, without some sort
    of way
To punish disobedience, in those who disobey?
So then, my boys, it's better, is it not, for you to fight
Whatever may be in you that prevents your doin' right?
And when you find how weak you are to conquer it
    alone,
Just ask the One to lend a hand who sits upon the
    Throne ;
And sure as you're a livin' boy, the help which you
    require
Will come as quick as messages on telegraphic wire ;
And you'll be sure He heard you by the sweet con-
    tent you feel,
And by your love for what is good, which is the
    Spirit's seal.
There'll come a time to most of you, somewhere along
    the route,
Where what we call "the cloudy days" will shut the
    sunshine out ;
And like enough, along with them, will come a sud-
    den dart,
And leave an awful achin' as it passes through your
    heart ;

And, may be, things may look awhile as though they
 all combine
And hedge you so completely round that hope can
 scarcely shine :
But, boys, if you'll be true to Him, and follow the old
 chart,
The darkness that is 'round about can't get into your
 heart;
His smile will make a sunshine that will send you on
 your way
As happy as the King's own son, through any kind of
 day.
Don't ever get a notion, whether life goes smooth or
 not,
That things are gettin' muddled, and your Father has
 forgot ;
Some things which you don't understand, may come
 because of sin,
And other things will happen, as a needed discipline;
But He who set you goin', in this journey, has His
 plan,
And He knows how to work it out for every boy or
 man.
And you just let Him have His way, and do as He
 commands,
And it won't take you long to see your Father under-
 stands.
And what a comfort it will be, and how 'twill give
 you rest,
To feel the sweet assurance that your Father knoweth
 best—

For you will come to places where 'twill trouble you
    to know,
Without some wiser counsel, where your feet had bet-
    ter go,
And then, because you love Him, and He knows you
    really try,
He'll let his spirit lead you, and " will guide you with
    His eye,"
And you shall feel His presence, that will fill your
    heart with song,
And when you would be timid, He will make you
    brave and strong ;
And when the flesh is weary with the burdens that
    you bear,
You'll find it very restful, if you'll spend a while in
    prayer ;
There's such a combination of the body with the soul,
That what pervades the spirit will at length pervade
    the whole.
But don't you get impatient, in your haste to be a
    man ;
But you enjoy your childhood just as fully as you can.
The years will, doubtless, seem to you, as movin'
    rather slow,
But they will be beyond your reach almost before you
    know,
For you can be as loyal as a boy as when a man,
For all your life is taken into God's eternal plan ;
And He is as delighted with a young life that's true
To meet the obligations that are given it to do,

As with the grey-haired fathers, who have fearlessly
    withstood

The shock of many battles, with what fortitude they
    could.

Be glad and happy : that don't mean that you're to
    have no care,

And cast on some one else the burdens which you
    ought to bear;

It simply means a spirit that will make you lend a
    hand

Wherever one is needed, and you've one at your com-
    mand,

And do it to be helpful ; not in a commercial way,

Drivin' a sort of bargain, just because you think 'twill
    pay ;

For that's the kind of spirit, if you let it get control,

Which fosters only selfishness, and surely dwarfs the
    soul,

And prompts the sort of actions which the most of you
    have seen,

And made you feel, instinctively, that they were small
    and mean ;

But strive to see what gladness and what sunshine you
    can fling

Across the path of others, and how you can make them
    sing,

Because your actions show them that you have a little
    care,

And feel a little sympathy with burdens that they bear.

Don't ever get a notion that you either know it all,

Or that you know so little that your chance is very
    small :
For if you get conceited, you have closed the avenue
Through which the best of knowledge could have ever
    come to you ;
And if you get despondent, by an underestimate
Of what there may be in you, then your chances are
    as great
That you won't ever come to much—or much won't
    come to you,
As if you thought you knew so much you hadn't
    much to do.
But you remember, always, that the ordinance of God,
For every person who would rise, is just to plod, and
    plod ;
But don't expect that you can rise by loadin' up your
    wings
With lots of either useless or with really harmful
    things;
And he who undertakes it, with some foolish habits,
    plods,
No matter what his energy, against a fearful odds.
Erect a lofty standard, boys, of what you mean to be,
And hold your course to reach it with a great per-
    sistency ;
Weak-hearted aims and purposes, however good they
    seem,
Will end about where they began, in just a pleasant
    dream.
You'll find a lot of places on your way, if you succeed,

To practice self-denial in the the things you think you
    need ;
And lots of other places where you'll find that you
    must be
A sort of tyrant to desires, and rule relentlessly.
But life is not a pastime, and success is not in dreams,
And self-denial not the cross, by half, it often seems :
You'll come to see beyond them, and go through them
    to your goal,
And find that your exalted aims have lifted up your
    soul.

A STRANGE COMBINE.

We've got an institution which, to use a common
    slang,
Has made a reputation as a sort of "jag shebang."
It takes the wrecks of manhood when they're ready to
    admit
That they are bound by appetite so strong they cannot
    quit,
But who have still a cravin' for the manhood that is
    slain,
If they can get their shackles off, and once be free
    again ;
And by a kind of treatment which is provin' a success,
Will send them back to liberty within a month, or less.

And then we've got another : it's an institution, too,
Which has a hundred branches which these patients
      must go through,
And graduate as drunkards, with an appetite so strong
That it becomes their master, and it doesn't take them
      long
Before they need the treatment of the "jag-cure" on
      the hill,
To make their bodies once again the servants of the
      will.
It takes a lot of money, too, to pass through its de-
      grees,
And pay the "incidentals" and the graduatin' fees.

And then we've got another, still, which stands be-
      hind them all ;
An institution without which the other two must fall,
And that's the family and home, with branches every-
      where,
To raise a crop of boys and girls, and have a lot to
      spare ;
About as farmers raise their crops for home use, and
      the mill,
Or cattle for their uses, and for some one else to kill:
The mothers raise their babies while the fathers give
      give consent
To sell them when they're old enough to bring the
      right per cent.

And there's a shrewdness in the scheme, which lets
    the boys mature
Before they're in the market, that the profits may be
    sure,
For boys of tender age would run a short race to their
    fall,
And yield but little revenue to Old King Alcohol.
And so the combination has decreed a strong decree,
That minors must not take the course in their minority.
Of course, there are precocious youths who do it, all
    the same,
But, then, the combination, in such cases, ain't to
    blame.

And these three institutions work together like a
    charm,
About as mill and slaughter-house go nicely with the
    farm,
With just this little difference, that profits which arise
Go mostly to the others, than who furnish the sup-
    plies.
While the saloon and "jag shebang" can pocket all
    the gains,
The institution back of them must suffer all the pains;
And yet they're in this strange combine, as it would
    seem, to stay,
If not for generations yet, at least for many a day.

POLITICAL EQUALITY.

Dot Voman's Demperance Union got von hifalutin'
    plan
To gif demselves bolitical eguality mit man ;
Dey advertise von sbeaker vhich dey get from off
    somevhere,
To dell our zity peoples how oppressed and crushed
    dey are ;
Dey hire de zity opera, which costs dem quite a sum,
Und scadder hantbills all aroun', invitin' us to come ;
Und if I don't get purty zick, my name ain't Uncle
    Zeke
If I don't takes mineself along to hear dot voman
    sbeak.

Bolitical eguality is vhat she sbeaks about,
Und I feel sort ov curious to zee vhat she makes out ;
I s'pose dot she vill tell us dot eguality denotes
Dot voman must be egual mit her husband vhen he
    votes ;
But vhedder she vill tell us dot to get de rights dey
    seek
De vimin must develop shust de same amount of
    "cheek,"
Und get de same eguality in all dose dirty dricks
Vhich makes de men successful in de field ov bolitics,
Is vhat I vants to hear her for ; I vant her to oxblain
How any such eguality will be for voman's gain.

De men vill nig and lie and fight about deir candidates,
Und mud each oder's characters at most indecent rates;
Dey buy und sell und even swop on every sort of plan
To garry out deir liddle schemes, und kill de oder man:
Und if eguality must mean dot vimin must eat dirt,
As many ov deir husbands do, deir morals might get
      hurt ;
For men—though dirty dogs demselves, und every-
      ting dot's mean—
Vill still insist dot vimin must be virtuous und clean.

Und if dey gits eguality, about vhich she vill sbeak,
I vonder if dey vouldn't get some tings dey didn't
      seek ;
Und if dey vould valk bravely through dem clouds ov
      backer smoke
To exercise de franchise, in de rights vhich dey in-
      voke.
Von ting is almost certain deir enfranchisement vould
      bring,
Dot old machine ov bolitics vould need a bigger ring,
Or else dem vhiskered bosses vould most likely hear a
      crash,
Und zee some schemes und swops ov deirs go shure
      enough to smash.

If voman's votes vould help redeem de nation's bolitics
From half de nasty schemin' und de vickedest ov
      tricks,
Ov vhich de men are guilty, ve can vell afford to say

To dose ve call our better halves, "You vote ; of
    course you may."
But, den, ve vouldn't do it, not by quite von little bit,
For half a dozen reasons ve're too vicked to admit.
If vimin got de franchise, und should use it as dey
    might,
Dey'd prove dot ve vas cowards, in not standin' for de
    right.

Ve can do vhat ve vant, as a peoples, every year,
Und only have such customs as ve rather vould be
    here ;
Ve makes such laws as suits us, und ve put such tings
    avay
As in our simple judgment vould be better than to
    stay :
But how 'twould look for vimin, who ve call de veak-
    er half,   .
To bring a reformation, und to give us men de langh.
Und dot is vhere it pinches, in dis country, vhich is
    free.
To let de vimin prove deir rights to have eguality.

THE BISHOP'S PRAYER.

(At the Opening of the World's Fair at Chicago.)

That was a great occasion, and its like was never
    known,
At least upon the continent we've learned to call our
    own.
A hundred thousand people, and with half as many
    more,
In one great sea of faces, whom the Bishop stood
    before ;
Gathered from out the families of men which underlie,
As its secure foundations, this great nationality.
And it was no small privilege for him to represent,
On such a great occasion, all the christian sentiment

PRAYER BY THE REV. BISHOP CHARLES H. FOWLER, D. D., LL. D.

At the Inaugural Exercises at Chicago.

(BUFFALO CHRISTIAN ADVOCATE.)

Almighty God, Our Heavenly Father, Thou art the
one only true God, eternal, immortal, invisible,
blessed over all forevermore. We come before Thee
to worship Thee, to render unto Thee thanksgiving,
to confess our helplessness, and to invoke thy blessing upon us. Thou art God. Thou hast created all
things. Thou hast made the world and all things
therein. Thou art Lord of heaven and earth. Thou
hast made of one blood all nations of men, for to dwell
on all the face of the earth, and hath determined the
times before appointed and the bounds of their habi-

Of not this continent alone, but of all Christendom,
Here where the mass of peoples are expected soon to
     come.
It was not as a single man that he was standin' there,
But he was voicin' sentiment of millions in his prayer.
He told the Lord a lot o' things, and told it eloquent,
Concernin' who and what He was, and of His gov-
     ernment,
And what He had been doin' since our nation had its
     birth,
By makin' it a beacon-light to nations of the earth ;
And how He had unfolded, from the scroll of history
     past,
His own divine conceptions, which were ripenin' so
     fast,
And bringin' in a heritage for all humanity,

---

tation.   As a people whom Thou hast exalted, we
worship Thee.   Before the majesty of Thy power and
the all-consuming glory of Thy presence, angels and
archangels veil their faces.   Thrones and dominions
and principalities and powers prostrate themselves.
Yet, we, the members of a fallen race, children of a
wayward family, urged by our dire necessities, en-
couraged by Thine unbreakable promises, emboldened
by Thine infinite love, inspired by Thy life-giving
spirit, and sheltered by the all-sufficient atonement,
press our way up to the very steps of Thy throne and
worship Thee, because Thou hast told us that in spite
of our littleness and in spite of our sinfulness we may
come, in the way Thou hast appointed, with boldness,
even to the mercy-seat.   Thou hast that supreme
power which is incapable of wearying, and that su-

Whose culminatin' glory should make all the nations
    free.
And then he asked God's blessings on the men of
    every land,
To hasten with more rapid strides a destiny so grand :
And if, when he had said all that, his prayer had
    ended then,
The christian hearts of every land would answer back
    "Amen !"
But he went on to tell the Lord what had been doin'
    there,
By those who had the management of this great
    comin' fair ;
What obstacles they'd conquered, and what triumphs
    they had won,

---

preme wisdom which is incapable of blundering, and
that supreme love which is incapable of upbraiding,
and we come unto Thee asking that Thou wilt
strengthen us in our weakness, guide us in our blindness, teach us in our ignorance, father us in our or-
phanage, pity us in our penitence, and save us in our
faith, and so help us that we may acceptably worship
Thee. We bless Thee, we praise Thee, we laud and
magnify Thy holy name.

We thank Thee for the overflowing goodness which
Thou hast manifested to us, exceeding abundant above
all that we can ask or think. We thank thee for the
revelation of Thyself in Thy Son to take away all sin,
in Thy Spirit to quicken every virtue, in Thy word to
dispel every superstition, in Thy providence to protect
from every evil. We thank Thee especially for Thy

Till much of what they'd started was at last so nearly
    done.
And then I noticed, for the first, the honored Bishop's
    lip
Had dropped its thread of narrative, and here began
    to skip :
He didn't tell the gracious Lord—as truthfully he
    might—
That through these same officials He (the Lord) had
    lost the fight,
And that these fair commissioners had hankered so for
    gold
That for it they'd consented that his Christ should
    here be sold ;
That here they had consented to the layin' of a snare
For every unsuspectin' foot that comes to see the fair ;

---

favoring providence, which has ordered the unfolding
of our history as a people, and the shaping of our destiny as a nation.   Thou didst keep this New World in
the thick clouds that surround thy purposes and didst
reserve it for the high honors of thy maturing kingdom.
In the fullness of time thou didst bring it to the
knowledge of men by the wisdom and prowess and
faith of Thy servant Columbus.   Thou didst so inspire
his mind and direct his thought by signs on the surface of the sea and by the flight of birds through the
depths of the air that the southern continent of the
Western hemisphere was open to southern Europe, and
this northern continent was preserved for another
people and another destiny.   Thus thou didst launch
upon the tide of history in the two continents of the
New World two new and great and mutually helpful

That here the gates of sin and vice might be thrown
    open wide,
To swallow down humanity which ventures on its tide;
That here the nations of the world might come to see
    the shame
Which these commissioners have brought on every
    christian name.
Ah, no ! he didn't tell the Lord this awful compromise
Which ought to bring the tears of shame to "all our
    weepin' eyes ;"
But after roundly laudin' all the workin's of their
    hand,
He asked the blessin' of the Lord on all that they had
    planned.
We would not wish to criticise—indeed, we would not
    dare—

---

nations. We thank Thee for thy favoring providence.
Thou didst speak to our fathers, heroic and great men,
men of prayer and power, and bade them come to this
open land and plant here in the wilderness great institutions for the elevation of the race, to consecrate
these vast valleys and endless plains to freedom, to
free ideas and free conscience, to the sanctity of the
private home and the inalienability of individual rights.
We thank Thee for the glorious history we have in-
herited ; for Crecy, for Smithfield, and for Marston
Moor, for Lexington and Fort Sumpter, for Yorktown
and Appomattox, these throbbing achievements of our
patriotism. We thank Thee for Washington and Lin-
coln, for Webster and Clay, for Jefferson and Jackson,
and for Grant—these beacon lights of the republic,
We thank thee for the mighty hosts of the heroic dead.

An exercise which we regard as sacred as a prayer ;
But with the facts so widely known, could he be
    ignorant
Of their official action, with congressional consent,
By which the greatest foe to God, and to the human
    race,
Became a partner in this fair, and took an honored
    place ?
Did he not know—this man of God, who told the
    Lord so much—
That alcoholic liquors hold a curse for all they touch ?
That these commissioners who heard the voicin' of
    his prayer
Had sold the " privilege " to men for sellin' liquors
    there ?

---

and for the priceless lesson they have taught us in
patriotism, in valor, in statesmanship, and in sacrifice.
We thank thee for 60,000,000 of free, heroic, patriotic
citizens ; for the open Bible, the open school, and the
open church ; for unprecedented growth, abundant
prosperity, multiplied inventions, unnumbered li-
braries, countless newspapers, many colleges, great
universities, ubiquitous benevolences, universal peace,
uninterrupted happiness, and untarnished honor. We
thank Thee for emancipated manhood and exalted
womanhood. We thank Thee for a free conscience,
by a free church, in a free State, for a free people.
For these precious and priceless blessings that make
life valuable and kindle quenchless hopes for this
world and for the world to come, we thank Thee.
    Now, O Lord our God, grateful for America, with

And now they ask, like Balak, that the man of God
    will bless

The good and bad which they have done, together, in
    a mess,

And sanctify the whole of it, that all the world may
    see

That nothin' dangerous can come of this great jubilee.

Balaam—though not a model of the prophets of his
    day—

Had loyalty enough to God to outwardly obey ;

And when he went, an hireling by a bribe from
    Balak's hand,

To stand before Jehovah, and bring back the Lord's
    command,

He dared not curse the people whom the Lord designed
    to bless,

---

her great republics and civil governments and free institutions, we ask thy continued blessings upon us.
Bless this nation, so heavily freighted with benedictions for mankind.   Bless the President of the
United States in his high official character.   Hear us
while we tarry to pray thy blessing on his family in
the stress of this hour.   While the warm sympathies
of the nation are poured into this our foremost and
representative home, may the comfort of thy grace
abound in that Christian family, and may thy tender
care preserve it unbroken for an example for many
years to come.   Bless the secretaries, the president's
constitutional advisers, the judges of the Supreme
Court, the senators, and congressmen of the United
States, the governors of the several commonwealths,
and all in official and responsible places.   Bless the

Nor change a word of his command, to make it more
  or less.
Oh, Balaam ! had you lived 'til now, the culture of
  to-day
Would tone those honest scruples of your heart, some-
  what, away ;
And like as not you'd get the bribe your poor heart
  coveted,
By changin' just a little of the words your Lord had
  said :
Too honest and too scrupulous for cultured times like
  these,
When prayers are said, and speeches made, the popu-
  lace to please ;
With not a word from Bishop, or from orator, to chide
The nation's representatives for throwin' open wide

---

officers of the army and of the navy, and the men who
stand for the defense of our flag. We pray Thee to
bless the women of America. Favored above their
sisters in all the world with open doors to varied
activities, with honorable recognition in the responsibilities of life and of character, and with large room in
society for the use and development of their gifts and·
acquirements and abilities, may they show to all the
women of the world the true dignity and glory of
Christian womanhood. We pray Thee to bless the
great body of our citizens, that they may improve and
perpetuate their patrimony. Bless the honorable and
learned professions in our land, that we may have
wise laws, just administrations, efficient remedies, be-
nign faiths, and helpful sciences. Bless the great body
of the wage-earners, and may labor and capital meet,

This world's great exposition, the more widely to
    proclaim
To all our guests from every land our peril and our
    shame.
We wonder what Elijah would have done had he been
    there,
And been the honored Bishop that was puttin' up that
    prayer :
Would he stretch out his sturdy hands—so mighty
    with the sword,
Over a compromise with hell, and utter not a word
Of scathin' reprimand for sin, so mighty to oppose
The kingdom of his Master, and so full of human woes ;
A thing indelicate to do, and sure to give offense,
And bring him lots of censure, as his worldly recom-
    pense ?

---

mingle, and thrive together on the basis of the New
Testament. Bless all the people from every land that
flow into our population, that all of every clime and
color and race may enjoy the blessings of righteousness and justice and protection and security under our
flag and on every yard of our soil. Bless us as a people
with enlarging intelligence and widening charities and
ever improving health and abounding liberality. Sanctify our homes, multiply our children, and continue
our prosperity. Above all things, make us eminent
for righteousness, a nation whose God is the Lord.
We pray thee to bless the president and general man-
ager of this exposition, and these commissioners, and
the men and women who have toiled amid many anx-
ieties and uncertainties for so many months to crown
this undertaking with success. May they have such

But if the many centuries which moved so slowly past
Leave him as much a hero now as when we saw him
    last,
We think these fair commissioners, most likely, would
    have heard,
From lips which were divinely touched, another kind
    of word
Than fulsome praise for deeds like these, which openly
    defy
The whole world's christian sentiment for all human-
    ity.
'Twas not a pleasant place to stand—that place he
    occupied
On that historic mountain, where he stemmed the
    swellin' tide
Of Israel's idolatry, and blew his trumpet blast,

---

wisdom and help from Thee for their difficult and delicate duties that they may deserve and receive the
grateful remembrance of their fellow-citizens. We
invoke Thy choicest blessings upon our guests, upon
those who come hither from distant lands and climes
to unite with us in this great enterprise, whether they
come from the rulers of the earth that they may see
and report what is doing in these ends of the world,
or to represent the arts that have matured through the
ages, or to set forth the triumphs of genius, the me-
chanical and industrial achievements that are en-
riching our times, we pray Thee to bless them and
keep them in health and safety while they are in our
midst. Keep their families and interests in their distant home, in peace and prosperity. May their return
to their homes be in safety and comfort, carrying

Which challenged all the hosts of Baal to measure
    strength at last
With him alone—a man of God—to a test that should
    require
That He who would be God, henceforth, should an-
    swer prayer by fire.
It was not courtin' favor of the king's authority
Which nerved his arm to strike that blow against
    idolatry,
Until his sword had drank the blood of every priest
    that led
Backslidin' Israel from God, and every one lay dead.
It was not pleasant to be chased, like hunted beast of
    prey,
An outlaw from the face of men, in peril night and
    day,

---

with them many kindly memories of this land and of
this city.

    Bless, we pray Thee, the great nations they repre-
sent. Bless the great Republic of France, that rising
sun of liberty on the shores of Europe. Bless the Republic of Switzerland, and the Republics of South
America, and the Republic of Mexico, and the Republics of Central America. May the torches they
hold up in the world never go out or burn dimly.
Bless the free government of Great Britain, with her
many and vast dependencies. Bless the lands of
Scandinavia with their heroic sons and daughters.
Bless the Empire of Germany with its advancing millions. Bless Italy, the cradle of Columbus, with her
history and her hopes. Bless genial and sunny Spain,
the land of Ferdinand and Isabella, the helpers of

And have a price put on his head, and have his only
    fare
What bread and meat a raven's wings and raven's
    beak could bear ;
And be for months and weary years most strictly a
    recluse,
And when not fed by ravens, livin' off a widow's cruse:
But God required some agency to go before that throng,
And thunder his anathemies against a mighty wrong,
And though he did not choose a work so difficult, but
    grand,
He could not shrink from doin' what he heard his
    Lord command.
And if I read my Bible right, no prophets have been
    sent
To wicked men or nations, to present a compliment

Columbus.   Bless Russia, the steady and fearless
friend of the United States, with her millions of subjects and of acres and of wants.   Bless Austria.
Bless China, populous China and Japan, and Corea
and Turkey and Africa, and all the nations of the
earth, whatever their form of government or type of
religion.   May the truths they hold be nourished.
May the light they have received grow brighter and
brighter to the perfect day.   May the liberties they
have reached be perpetuated and multiplied till all the
nations of the earth shall be freed from error, from
superstition, and from oppression, and shall enjoy the
blessing of righteousness, of liberty, of equality, and
of brotherhood, with Thy perpetual favor.   We pray
Thy blessing upon America in an especial manner,
according to her responsibilities.   May she come up

For layin' snares adroitly, with so much that may be
        good,
That to the unsuspectin' they are little understood,
And hence they fall an easy prey, while yieldin' to the
        charm
Of pleasure's silken voice that sings, their scruples to
        disarm.
What prophets were in times of old, as it appears to
        me,
Those who stand nearest to the Lord in modern times
        should be ;
Not courtin' favor with the world, but mighty for de-
        fense
Of that for which they're chosen and sent out by Prov-
        idence ;

---

to the character thou requirest of her.   May she accomplish the exalted work of helping to draw the
nations of the earth into a close and friendly brotherhood that shall practice the arts of peace and go forth
to war no more forever.   May our republic grow
stronger in the hearts of the people and in the respect
of sister nations as the ages roll by.   May she grow
rich in intelligence, in educational resources, in the
fine arts, in the sciences, in the productive industries,
and in the great wealth of noble and righteous character that shall make her the friend of all nations, to
whom the needy nations shall turn for help, the be-
wildered for counsel, the weak for protection, the
strong for wisdom, and all for fellowship ; and may
she fill the world for future ages with the gladness and
glory of our Christian civilization.

The truth of God, all righteousness, and strike their
        hardest blows
At *those who take the foremost rank among his Mas-*
        ter's foes.
This prayer was great, not only in the manner which
        it plead,
But great in its omissions, in the things it left unsaid;
Not one in all that throng would know, from hearin'
        while he prayed,
That any giant wrongs were done, or compromises
        made ;
Or would suspect, from hearin' him address a throne
        of grace,
That these whom he was blessin' had defied Him to
        His face ;

O Almighty God, we are gathered here within these walls and within these gates from our national capital, and from every city and section of our wide domain, and from all the lands of the earth, to acknowledge Thee ; and in Thy name, and in the name of the government of the United States, and in the name of the people of the United States, to dedicate these buildings and these grounds to the uses and purposes of the World's Columbian Exposition. We pray Thy blessing upon this undertaking, that it may bring glory to Thy name and benedictions to mankind.

Now, O Lord our Father, we pray Thy blessing upon this multitude. In Thy great mercy forgive the sins of each of us and bless us with eternal salvation. As this assembly will scatter and soon be gone, may each one be ready to stand in that great assembly

That christian sentiment had plead, but always plead
    in vain,
That this great exposition might be clean from such a
    stain ;
Or that the Bishop's heart was grieved because of that
    defeat,
Which let the devil—for a while—usurp his Master's
    seat.
I don't know as I'm orthodox, because I must declare
That my poor heart revolted, when I read the Bishop's
    prayer.
His askin' God to sanction what these Godless men
    had planned,
Without exceptin' anything, was more than I could
    stand ;
And I began to wonder if the Bishop really meant
To ask the Lord Almighty if He wouldn't give con-
    sent
To ruin man and womanhood, for whom His Son had
    died,
Because the " privilege " would pay for space it occu-
    pied ;

------

which shall gather before Thy throne, and be per-
mitted to hear the supreme sentence, "Well done,
enter thou into the joy of thy Lord."   And unto
Thee, our God and our Father, through Him who is
the friend of sinners, will we, with the angels that
stand about the throne, ascribe "blessing and glory
and wisdom and thanksgiving and honor and power
and might forever and ever.   Amen."

Or whether—unbeknown to him—in his embarrass-
        ment,
Another Spirit than the one by whom he had been
        sent,
Had, for this great occasion, caused his memory to slip,
To spare these men the chastisement that might es-
        cape his lip ;
Or whether, for the moment, it was takin' such a
        lead,
That when the prayer was printed, it would almost
        seem to read
Like after dinner speeches, which are framed for men
        to hear,
Instead of bein' framed to reach the King Eternal's
        ear.
It's not for me to answer, but I almost think I know
That sanction won't be given—if the Bishop meant it
        so :
The God of all creation, while he loves His people's
        praise
Is neither coaxed or flattered to endorse their crooked
        ways,
For wrong—in all disguise—is wrong, in places high
        or low,
And everybody, soon or late, will harvest what they
        sow.

A LITTLE HOGGISH.

The same congress that refused even to consider the ravages of the liquor traffic, appropriates $100,000 a year to investigate hog cholera: $100,000 outlay to save swine from infection; $100,000,000 income to spread contagion in the way of the boys.—*Western Advocate.*

We wouldn't minify the hog: the place he occupies
Would bother us to substitute, in matter of supplies;
From bristles down to rooter he's important to the
    state,
And well deserves a little thought from those who
    legislate.
He puts a lot of money in the tills of Uncle Sam,
And furnishes his table with his bacon and his ham;
He shortens half his pie-crust, and he greases half
    his gear,
And saves a lot of friction to the nation every year.

It wouldn't do to leave him to the happenings of fate,
When he is so important to the progress of the state;
A hundred thousand dollars we can well afford to pay
To keep his mortal enemy—the cholera—away;
And then a hundred thousand to investigate the cause,
And hedge himself and family about with stringent
    laws,
Regardin' both his diet and condition of his pen,
Because he's such a factor in the busy lives of men.

But here's the strange condition : there is nothin' in
    the health
Of all the hogs in Christendom, as elements of wealth,
Or elements of danger, as a merchandise or meat,
Except as they're related to the mouths of men that
    eat ;
And where's the decent logic of an economic plan
Which sets a greater value on a hog than on a man?
Since hogs would be as valueless as stiles upon the pen,
Except as they contribute to the common wants of men.

His value as a factor in the nation's merchandise
Is measured only by the need his family supplies.
Preserve the health and lives of men, in this or any
    land,
And hogs increase in value by increasin' the demand ;
But such a simple axiom—so plain to any fool—
Seems out of reach of statesmen of the politician's
    school,
Whose wisdom—as it's outlined by their latest policy—
Is killin' off the eaters, while increasin' the supply.

They legislate to spare the hog, because he represents
A value they can figure up in dollars and in cents ;
They also legislate for men, but do it with the brains
Which only seem to calculate along financial gains,
And that in superficial ways ; for if they calculate
They'll find a man is better than a hog, to any state,
And has a market value—if they know enough to
    weigh—
Above him in the matter of investments that will pay.

It looks a little hoggish, does it not, to legislate
To spend the nation's money freely to investigate
What causes pigs and hogs to die, and stop it if they
     can,
And then not spend a dollar to protect the life of man?
But they are doin' worse than that—you call it what
     you will :
They legislate a policy which rather aims to kill—
Not pigs and hogs, but living men; and does it day
     by day,
And then are blind enough to think such policy can
     pay.

We called it hoggish policy, but we will take it back,
Because it slanders all the race of bristles, white or
     black :
They may be heavy eaters, but, if they're let alone,
Rarely become so vicious that they will destroy their
     own.
The devil may be in them, but not by direct descent,
For not a single one was left of those in whom he
     went,
But every one of them were drowned, and buried in
     the sea,
With not a single scion left as their posterity.

But he is in the policy which lays its snare for boys,
By countless open ways of death, and countless sly
     decoys,
With legislative sanction, or in spite of their decrees,
And drowns a mighty herd of them in alcoholic seas ;

While those who represent the victims gravely sit in
        state,
And reach no hand to rescue them, but leave them to
        their fate ;
Nay, rather, lend their voice and vote, the multitude
        to swell,
By pavin' this, the broadest way, to the widest gates
        of hell.

THE LAST ASSESSMENT.

(The $390 levied upon the prostitutes of the city,
and paid into the city treasury, recently.)

How virtue is exalted, and the moral atmosphere
Is fumigated by a tax, collected once a year !
How decency has been enthroned, and lust has been
        forestalled,
And prostitution is rebuked till utterly appalled ;
And white-winged innocence returns, and spreads her
        hands in haste
Over the scarlet records of the past, which are unchaste,
And how the loathsome current of diseases have been
        stayed
From preying on our populace, because this tax was
        paid !

How manhood has been dignified by taxin' human lust
To run our city government—proclaimin' it as just ;
And that by laws enacted and administered to raise
A revenue of decency from such abhorrent ways :
And what an index finger of the moral estimate
Which men attach to virtue, do these taxes indicate,
When they by legislation or judicial acts proclaim
That cities shall be richer for their houses of ill-fame !

We dare not call it beastly, for all animals would cry
That they were bein' slandered, and pronounce the
     charge a lie.
Perhaps it may be manly for the sex which has control
To legalise the business for a portion of the toll,
And levy on the earnings of the sex without a voice
Whatever dividends they like, without consent or
     choice,
Provided they enjoy it ; but it takes a lot o' "gall"
To parcel out these dividends to benefit us all.

THE CHOIR'S NEW "FAD."

We s'pose we shouldn't be surprised at anything we
     see
Along the line of fashion in high-toned society ;
For there's a lot of people who have little else to do,
Than make themselves conspicuous by doin' somethin'
     new.

And there's a larger number still who love to follow
    on
In almost any sort of ways where high-toned feet have
    gone ;
Whose "acme" of ambition seems to be a zealous
    "ad"
In one way and another for the newest kind of "fad."

But one would hardly look to see these senseless
    "fads" invade
The sanctuary of the Lord, and there make their pa-
    rade,
And least of all would one expect—if they were any-
    where—
That they would thrust their nonsense in the solemn
    act of prayer.
But, somehow, they have done it ; and the organist
    must play
Some soft chords on the organ, for the minister to
    pray ;
As though a prayer ascended to the presence of the
    Lord,
With more of an acceptance for the playin' of a chord.

They've got a scripture warrant that the instruments
    may play
To help along the singin', but not help the preacher
    pray ;
For prayer is talkin' to the Lord, and such a solemn
    act

Needs concentration of the thoughts, with nothin' to
    distract.
The buzzin' of an organ, playin' chords for dancin'
    feet,
Or blendin' with the singin' may be altogether meet ;
But playin' chords for preachers, while they raise
    their voice in prayer,
Strikes us as bein' somethin' of a different affair.

For when a congregation would address the great " I
    Am,"
They ought, at least, to do it without any sort of sham,
For He is never silly, to mistake such empty plays
For honest supplication, or for simple, heart-felt
    praise.
When He has been so gracious, in the months and
    years gone by,
To recognize our services, and keep us company,
It seems, indeed, it seems to us, as bein' quite too bad,
To sandwich in our worship, such an empty, silly
    " fad."

UNCLE ALVIN AT NIAGARA.

"The last excursion of the year," I read the other
    day,
Affordin' opportunity to see grand old Niagara ;
And for a dollar and a half, to go up there and back,
And see the sights, and ride above two hundred miles
    of track,
Seemed like we'd get our money's worth, if we could
    get away,
And leave the farm and kitchen cares behind us for a
    day.
We'd been a-wantin', all these years, to go and see
    the falls,
But, somehow, when the chances came there'd be so
    many calls
For both our time and money, that the chances slipped
    away,
While year climbed on the top of year, 'til we are
    growin' gray ;
And still the cares we have to meet are such a clingin'
    kind,
It's often mighty difficult to slip them off behind,
And dump them in a heap somewhere, or lay them on
    a shelf,
While we get out from under, and can slip off by
    ourself.

But nature seemed to favor us ; the season was so fine
We got our summer's work along a bit ahead of time ;
And nothin' seemed a-crowdin', like, and coaxin' to
    be done,
As is the case too frequently, to keep us on the run ;
And Nancy hadn't been away, exceptin' to the fair,
To loosen up the constant strain of daily wear and tear
Of wrestlin' with problems which perplex a woman's
    brain,
And keep her fingers busy, and her muscles on the
    strain,
For such a long time back that I'm almost ashamed
    to tell,
And if I really wanted to, I couldn't very well ;
And I, myself, had worked so long, as farmers have to
    do,
To keep the work from snarlin', like, and keep it
    payin', too,
That I was glad to see a chance to lay aside the strain
Which makes the years to tell on me as well as Nancy
    Jane ;
And when I read the notice, why, it seemed to strike
    us so,
That both of us together said, "I guess we'd better
    go."
And so the thing was settled, and we'd picked our
    grapes and plums
To be ahead of frost or thieves, provided either comes ;
For frosts may be expected almost any pleasant night,
And thieves, if not expected, are so plenty that they
    might ;

And Nancy had our luncheon baked, and I had bought
        some cheese,
And she had found a paste-board box, as handy as
        you please
To put our picnic dinner in ; so when the mornin'
        came,
We wasn't in a flurry, and the both of us to blame,
But had our things in order, and it didn't take us long,
(For, somehow, things move faster when the heart is
        full of song)
To fix ourselves and get to town, and put our nag
        away,
And say a benediction on our cares, for just a day,
And get ourselves among the crowd that was a-comin'
        there,
Just as the whistles blew for seven—with half an hour
        to spare,
In buyin' tickets, shakin' hands, and tryin' hard to
        wait,
Without a little query if the train would not be late.
But just at seven-thirty, sure enough, somebody
        roared,
As only a conductor can, and shouted "all aboard."
And then the engine gathered up, as if to do her best,
And after snortin' once or twice, she started for the
        west.
The day was all that one could wish—no suffocatin'
        air,
No dust a-lightin' in your eyes, and flyin' everywhere;
No sombre clouds all overhead, begettin' thoughts of
        gloom

To people passin' under them, like crape about a
    room,
But nature seemed a-crowdin' all creation with the
    gold
Of her September loveliness, as full as it could hold,
And everywhere one turned their eyes, they fell upon
    a scene
Of purple, gold and scarlet hues, a-blendin' in the
    green ;
And I don't think if she had been a-doin' it for pay,
To make our pleasure perfect, she could make a finer
    day.
We stopped at every station that we found along the
    road,
And people kept a-comin', 'til the cars got such a load
That every time the engine tried to gather up the slack,
Before she got them all to move her wheels would slip
    the track ;
But when she got a-goin' how she made the cinders
    fly,
And kept the trees and fences just a-jumpin' in your
    eye.
And after all her stoppin', and her startin' up so slow,
She took us on as fast as I or Nancy cared to go ;
And everything went on as smooth and regular as
    rhyme,
And got us to the cataract as advertised—on time.
Of course, we bein' strangers there, not knowin'
    where to go,
We joined the stream of people, and we followed in
    the flow

In the direction of the falls which were not far away,
Till all of us stood face to face with old Niagara.
We were delightfully surprised, on goin' from the
      train,
To meet some friends of other years and shake their
      hands again ;
And they appeared as gratified at meetin' thus as we ;
And so, by mutual consent, we kept them company,
And had the double pleasure of enjoyin' all the roar
And seein' all the sights we could, and talkin' "by-
      gones" o'er.
Of course, we pointed for the park, for what else
      could attract
The thought of any one so near this monster cataract?
And got our first installment on the pleasures of the
      day
By takin' in a little of the sights of Niagara.
And after viewin' it awhile, the granduer of the sight
(Or else it was our forenoon's ride) had whet our ap-
      petite,
Till we concluded it was best to find a nice retreat,
Where we could keep on seein' while we visited and
      eat.
Of course, we'd seen it all before, from every point of
      view,
As well as photographs could show—and they are very
      true ;
But lookin' at a picture, though as true as true can be,
Is different from lookin' at a live reality.
And here, spread out before us, was the wildest poet's
      dream,

Wrought out of rock and water-fall, in noonday's
  brightest beam ;
The wonder of all ages, which all people come to see,
And carry on forever thoughts of its immensity.
We saw the whole of it we could, and tried to realize
The magnitude of what was there revealed before our
  eyes :
But as we went from point to point, to gather some-
  thin' new,
And saw such granduer everywhere, the more our
  wonder grew,
Till we, at length, were conscious of a sort of name-
  less awe,
While standin' in the presence of the mighty things
  we saw.
We thought we might describe them some, but how
  shall feeble pen
Convey the grandeur that was here to minds of other
  men ?
Word-pictures, like the photograph, may all be more
  than true,
But when the words exhaust themselves, not half is
  brought to view ;
The eyes and soul must both be there to fully comprehend
This panorama, where so much of power and beauty
  blend.
And when they drink in all they can, of Nature's
  great display,
They'll find their wonder growin', as the days shall
  glide away:

Their thoughts will keep on runnin', and unfoldin',
    more and more,
The awful power behind it all, as never seen before ;
And here, there's such a feelin' comes a stealin'
    through the heart,
That makes a person shudder at the paucity of art.
What man in such a presence could be tempted to be
    vain,
Who has the sensibilities of cultured heart and brain?
Almost, it makes a person feel as if he would repeat
That act of Moses when he took the shoes from off
    his feet ;
For, surely, God is in this place, and blind must that
    one be,
Who can not see, or hear His voice, in this immensity.
We climbed upon a crest of rock, beside the foamin'
    sheet,
Which lashed itself to frenzy, as it hurried past our
    feet,
And cast our eyes far up the stream—a half a mile or
    more,
To see it pourin' off the sky, it seemed, from shore to
    shore,
In rumble, tumble, headlong haste, dispensin' sound
    and spray,
And flecked with foamin' madness, as it dashes down
    it's way ;
Already down a hundred feet from where it caught
    our eye,
A half a mile above us, where it pours from off the
    sky,

It seemed to turn to whiteness, as it bows itself to go
From off the fearful precipice into the depths below ;
How far, we dare not try to tell, and scarcely even
     guess,
But, possibly, a thousand feet, or somethin' more or
     less,
For where it reached the surface of the water, down
     below,
Was scarcely more than half, perhaps, the distance it
     must go ;
And what impresses me as strange about this water-
     fall
Was at the surface where it poured, which scarcely
     boiled at all,
But simply had some riffles, which were slightly
     flecked with foam,
And boats, conveyin' passengers, may on it safely
     come
So close to where the mighty sheet of foamin' water
     fell,
It almost seemed to those on shore (incredulous to
     tell)
As if a lusty hand stretched out from off the vessel's
     brow,
Might catch a hand-full of it's foam, or touch it, any-
     how ;
And certainly, it sailed so close as to be hid away,
Almost entirely from view, enveloped in the spray.
And one can form a faint idea how deep these waters
     go,

When told that they appear again two miles, and
    more, below,
And form the whirlpool rapids, where it's pent-up
    power appears,
The wonder of all continents, and wonder of all years.
And then our thoughts went climbin' back, along the
    lengthy chain
Of mighty inland waters, which this river helps to
    drain ;
Far up, and up to mountain peaks, with everlastin'
    snow,
And into hidden fastnesses, as far as thought could go,
To find the sources, if we could, that furnish it's sup-
    ply,
Whose everlastin' runnin' doesn't seem to run it dry.
But if we marked out all we found, 'twould make a
    mighty map
Of rivulets and little streams, convergin' to the lap
Of nature's biggest basin, with Niagara for a spout,
To form a sort of safety gauge, and let it's surplus out.
But with such map before us, one could hardly feel
    the beat
Of nature's great big pulsin' heart, which throbs be-
    neath our feet,
And sends it's countless veins so thick, that, tap it
    where we will,
In plain or valley, gorge or cliff, on mountain top or
    hill,
We'll hardly miss of strikin' one, and seein' water
    flow,

Without our knowin' whence they come, or whither
    they will go.
Oh, Nature ! thou art mystery ; explain thee as we
    will ;
The little that we know of thee is like a tiny rill, .
Whose waters quickly lose themselves in such a vast
    array,
As pour down so incessantly over old Niagara.
We wondered where these waters were, while He who
    formed their bed
Which they have traveled over for so long, with noisy
    tread,
And out of what He formed the rocks, and how He
    laid them so,
That they resist so long and well their forces, as they
    flow
With such momentum that we know that for them to
    resist,
From age to age, as they have done, these blows from
    Nature's fist,
The masonry must far excel the work of human hands,
And glorify His workmanship, because His structure
    stands.
And then, again, we questioned, but we didn't calcu-
    late
How long the fluids in her veins require to circulate,
And just how often every drop, since first her pulses
    beat,
Have jumped this awful cataract and made the round
    complete :

But more than once, we fancied, and, perhaps, more
    than we dream,
These waters make the whole round trip, and dash
    along this stream ;
And that which formed the coffee which we drank but
    yesterday
May form a part of this great flood some time not far
    away ;
For Nature never wastes a drop, wherever it may go,
In veins of men or animals, or in the plants that grow,
But keeps an eye on all she has, and never loses track,
And after patient waitin' she is sure to get it back.
We didn't go to Canada, for sights on our own side
Kept us tremendous busy and our time all occupied ;
But we kept glancin' over, and the sight of it brought
    back
Some saddened memories of times when brothers
    clothed in black
Thought it was Heaven, as, indeed, it often proved
    to be ;
For there, if they could cross this stream, they might
    at last be free.
Ah, memory ! how she spreads her wings at sight of
    Canada,
And takes us back to other days, before our locks
    were gray,
When refugees from slavery, with blood-hounds on
    their track,
Were hunted, like the wildest beasts, to catch and
    carry back ;

But with the north star for their guide, they risked,
    as well they might,
The teeth of their pursuers, for the sake of Heaven's
    right
For every man to own himself, subject, alone, to God,
And fling defiance, when they could, to tyrant mas-
    ter's nod.
Thank God, the prayed-for day is here, when only
    memory
Can find a man in manacles, from sea across to sea,
And purged from our iniquity, we spread our washen
    hands
To help the cause of liberty to spread throughout all
    lands.
The rocks on either side suggest that down the past,
    somewhere,
These falls were miles and miles below the place
    where now they are,
And by the water's mighty force were eaten back, and
    worn
The chasm as we see it now, with edges fringed and
    torn.
And fancy floated down the stream to where the falls
    began,
A thousand ages farther than the history of man,
And saw it eatin', inch by inch, the porous rock away,
And climbin' slowly toward the place it occupies to-
    day.
We saw some sturdy relics, through the sunbeams and
    the mist,

That whispered from the bottom, where their sides
    were bein' kissed,
That told as plain as language could that they had
    occupied
A higher place than they do now, a-holdin' up the
    tide,
Just where it makes its final leap, 'til on a certain day
It lost the grip which held it up, and then it fell away,
And lies to waste for ages more, 'til beaten into sands,
It goes to join its comrades off in other seas or lands.
Well, when we'd made Goat Island from its many
    points of view,
And visited "Three Sisters," as all visitors should
    do,
For there we got the grandest sight of all the grand
    display,
And that does not belittle all the others seen that day;
We thought that we, my friend and I (the women
    wouldn't go),
Must see how old Niagara looked when seen from
    down below ;
And so we took the railroad car—it wasn't quite a
    train—
Which carries people up and back by cable rope and
    chain ;
And down and down and down we rode, 'til bottom
    came at last,
And out of "the incline" we went, and down the
    steps we passed,
And stood at length among the rocks, the rainbows
    and the mist,

And felt, as never in our lives, that we were bein'
    kissed
By Nature's own delightful lips, and baptised with
    her spray,
Which knows no times or seasons, but unchanged,
    from day to day ;
And felt the throbbin' of her heart, and heard her
    voice repeat,
In tones as loud as thunder, and delivered at our feet,
That taught our hearts a lesson which we wouldn't
    like to miss,
That none but she herself can show how truly great
    she is.
Then up and up and up we gazed, to see the foamin'
    sheet
Which poured in such a volume down so closely to
    our feet
That only for the mist, we thought, we might ap-
    proach so nigh
Our hands could touch the torrent that was pourin'
    from on high ;
And we were goin' toward it, for the breeze took all
    the spray,
For quite a little moment, just across the other way,
Till we were almost close enough, when, quicker 'n
    you can tell,
The breeze turned back toward us again, then how
    the water fell !
And how we scampered through it, for we hadn't
    rubber clothes,

And didn't relish gettin' wet, as you may well sup-
    pose.
But such a sight as we beheld beggars all words I
    know,
To tell of all the grandeur of Niagara from below.
The sun, in all his brightness, was just pourin' in his
    beams,
And gildin' everything it touched with rainbow-tinted
    gleams ;
And countless diamonds, bright as real, sparkled in
    its rays,
And made the mighty sheet of foam resplendent with
    its blaze,
While all the mist about us was a rainbow-tinted
    mass,
Which looked as though it was composed of floatin'
    dust of glass.
I sighed to be a painter, then, so I might take away,
That I might see it when I would, the scenes I saw
    that day ;
And then I thought that paint and brush and human
    skill combined,
In their best combinations, were like beauty to the
    blind,
Compared with this, where Nature's brush makes
    everything to glow
And pulse and sparkle in the light with life and
    beauty so.
But I stood there and drank it in, again and yet again,
That I might photograph it all back somewhere in
    my brain,

And carry back to old Steuben, as perfect as I might,
A picture in my memory of this transcendent sight.
And then we jumped on "the incline," and back to
      earth we flew,
So fast that if we'd struck the roof we must have
      broken through ;
But luckily we didn't, and we reached the solid
      ground,
Just dampened with Niagara's mist, but wholly safe
      and sound ;
And when we'd found the better halves which we had
      left behind,
We took the "Whirlpool Rapids" cars, some other
      sights to find ;
And sure enough, we found a sight—Suspension bridge
      and all—
For 'way down here, two miles away, comes up the
      waterfall
From under such a surface that no one would ever
      dream
That far below its tranquil bosom boiled a turbid
      stream,
Made strong, and even crazy, by the fearful plunge it
      took,
And under whose momentum even solid mountains
      shook.
And who can wonder at it, that it's boilin' waters
      whirl,
And leap, and plunge, and foam, and roar, and swirl,
      and swirl, and swirl,

For miles and miles, between the rocks, piled up in
    solid walls,
On either side, but narrower than just below the falls.
No boat could ride this seethin' tide and come intact
    below,
Nor livin' thing, which has not fins, would dare at-
    tempt to go.
One man, I read, so lost his head that he thought he
    could swim
These awful rapids, years ago, but 'twas the last of
    him.
Others have tried to make the ride in air tight bar-
    rel boats,
But one such ride has satisfied as far as history quotes;
Their inward groans and pommelled bones have cured
    their thirst for fame,
If such a feat they must repeat to blare abroad their
    name.
No man of sense tempts Providence by riskin' life
    and limb,
When his success can neither bless mankind, nor
    honor Him.
Fools often do to show their nerve, or possibly, their
    skill,
Defyin' laws without a cause, except themselves to
    kill :
But then, their loss is but the dross burned out of
    better ore,
And all mankind that's left behind is richer than be-
    fore;

Their vanity, perhaps, may be the wings of God's
    great mill,
To winnow chaff from out the half He wants His bins
    to fill;
At any rate they rid the State, perhaps their friends
    beside,
Of grave responsibilities, and room they occupied.
We reached the rapids, where they start, but this time
    had to pay
A half a dollar each to ride the cable-chain railway.
The other, at the falls above, belongin' to the State,
Charged just a dime, for down and back, with dis-
    tance just as great.
And why should not the State control all avenues that
    lead
To sights which all men ought to see, instead of hu-
    man greed?
Here, where the sons of men should come with rev-
    erential tread,
And witness what the Lord is doin', with uncovered
    head.
And what a comment on the vice of human avarice,
To thrust itself before the world in such a place as
    this.
That man of old, who sold his Lord to gratify his
    greed,
But knew enough to hang himself, has left a lot of
    seed ;
No place so sacred anywhere, in earth, or heaven, or
    hell,

But that, if they possessed the power, they'd fence it
    off to sell.
Oh, lust for gain ! what countless sins are rappin' at
    your door ;
While men are growin' rich and fat from off God's
    hungry poor,
And how the ears of justice must grow weary with
    their cry,
And how the sword of recompense must flourish bye
    and bye ;
And how must hell enlarge herself, to let the people
    in,
Whose thought of human brotherhood is swallowed
    by this sin,
And how the patient sons of God can well afford to
    wait
His careful re-adjustments, whether comin' soon or
    late ;
No balances so fine as His, to weigh the acts of men,
And no dishonest fingers 'round to do the weighin'
    then,
But simple justice, pure and sweet, His balances will
    weigh,
No matter who goes up or down on re-adjustment day.
Two iron bridges span the gulf at this point, side by
    side,
Transportin' passengers and freight across the boilin'
    tide.
A train crossed old Suspension bridge while we stood
    underneath,

And while our eyes gazed up at it we almost held our
    breath.
We stood where we could lay our hands upon an up
    stream guy,
And feel the tremble of the train movin' across the
    sky,
And thought of that terriffic plunge that movin' train
    must take,
With all the people on it, if the tremblin' bridge
    should break ;
And what a little difference their splashin' in the
    stream
Would make a moment afterward, as far as it would
    seem.
Hearts might be bleedin' somewhere else, and homes
    be desolate,
Because the snappin' of a wire released them to their
    fate ;
But little would Niagara feel of any sort of care,
For persons or for property which might be buried
    there.
Here in the presence of such power, a thoughtful
    mind will see
The contrast in it's awful force, and man's impotency ;
And likely feel, as well he might, desire begin to start,
That He who moves before His eyes, might dwell
    within His heart.
We couldn't take in all the sights in one short half a
    day
There is around Niagara, but we brought some things
    away,

That give a richer tinge to life, and broaden out the
      mind,
And make one's spirit spread her wings to see what
      she can find
In other spaces, which, to us, are thus far unexplored,
Which Nature's God, and ours as well, so lavishly
      has stored,
Not simply in the realm of sense, where careless feet
      may tread,
But in the spirit's wider range, around, and overhead,
And more than all, within the soul, of elements we
      need
To perfect man and womanhood in spirit and in deed.
The six hours that we had to spend were fairly occu-
      pied,
Till eyes as well as body lagged, and we felt satisfied
To loiter at the station for the comin' of the train,
And leave the wonders we had missed until we come
      again.
Of course, the hundred miles and more we had to
      ride at night
Had in them more of weariness than they had of de-
      light ;
But steam makes way in night or day, and covers dis-
      tance fast,
And every scream of whistlin' steam proclaimed a
      station passed ;
And dropped us down in our own town precisely half-
      past ten,
And 'twasn't long 'til Nancy Jane and I were home
      again.

And on the whole I think it proved the most delight-
    ful day,
For both our minds and hearts, at least, we ever spent
    away :
Our bodies suffered some fatigue and felt a little wear,
Which, even at our age, we think a few days will
    repair ;
But nothin' can eliminate impressions that were made
While viewin' the magnificence of Nature's great
    cascade ;
And often, in our memories, we'll see its torrents pour,
And rainbows painted on the mist, and hear its pon-
    d'rous roar,
And see its rapids swirlin' down, and bridges in the
    air,
And see its ragged greystone rocks projectin' every-
    where ;
And not unfrequently, perhaps, will fancy stroll away,
And weave its webb of romances about old Niagara.
Of course, we don't begrudge the day, or money that
    we spent,
But always shall congratulate ourselves because we
    went ;
And like as not, if we keep well, we'll take another
    ride,
To see how all these wonders look seen from the other
    side :
But life is so uncertain that, instead of goin' there,
Perhaps we'll make the journey where the many
    mansions are,

And see that other river, more majestic in its flow,
Where trees with healin' in their leaves upon its bor-
     ders grow ;
And see how grand the Capitol of Earth and Heaven
     will be,
And see the King, and great white Throne, in all
     their majesty ;
And listen to the music of the multitudes who sing
Their loudest, sweetest choruses in honor of their King.
The sights of earth are wonderful, but don't at all
     compare
With what we may expect to see when we get over
     there ;
And if these fill us with delight, what rapture must
     it be
To stand where God has done his best, and all His
     glory see ?
If He who scatters such delights along our earthly
     way,
To spice our lives with gladness for the little time we
     stay,
What may we not expect to find where He has done
     His best
To make the place delightful, for His own eternal rest.

HOW UNCLE ALVIN LOST HIS WHISKERS

Not many folks who see me now, and find me lookin'
 so,
Would think I've had as nice a beard as any man
 could grow ;
But that's a fact, for from the time when I had passed
 eighteen,
I had as comely whiskers as is very often seen ;
Not coarse and stiff as bristles, like so many that you
 see,
But fine and soft, and curly, like, as any need to be ;
And yet I wasn't proud of them, because I wouldn't
 shave,
But couldn't see the common sense of bein' such a
 slave ;
For nature made the beard to grow upon the human
 face,
To add as much to comfort as to give an added grace ;
And hackin' with a razor is about as barbarous
As almost any foolish thing that's ever charged to us.
If nature should forget—for once—and make a man
 without,
I think he'd try most anything to cause a beard to
 sprout ;
And then, if after coaxin' so, till nature should suc-
 cumb

And granted what he'd asked her for, and kindly gave
    him some,
What would she think, if after that he should become
    a slave,
And give her such a grave affront as goin' on to
    shave ?
A beard, which nature gave us is a manly thing to
    wear,
As it is clearly womanly to go with faces bare.
It wouldn't make a man of her if she should grow a
    beard,
Nor would he be a woman if his whiskers disap-
    peared.
And "apin" one another doesn't greatly signify,
Since we don't very well succeed, no matter how we
    try.
Well, I had practiced what I preached for thirty years
    and more,
And was contented, if not proud, with whiskers that I
    wore ;
But when I least suspected any grave calamity,
I made a small investment, which was all of that to
    me.
'Twas just an ulster overcoat, a kind of brown and
    gray,
That answers very nicely just for wearin' every day ;
And it was thick and heavy, and would keep a person
    warm
In almost any weather, from the wind, or in a storm ;
And had a lusty collar that would cover up my ears,

And made me feel the winter less than I had done for
    years ;
And with it on, and collar up, was such a cozy place,
That I most always wore it so, turned up against my
    face.
But long before the winter frosts had took themselves
    away,
I noticed, with no small regret, my beard was gettin'
    gray ;
And in a little while I saw that it was growin' thin,
And soon it wasn't any good for hidin' up my chin.
But all the while 'twas gettin' gray, and fallin' out so
    fast,
I never once mistrusted, 'till the danger line was
    passed,
That this was all a comin' from the overcoat I wore,
'Til, when the beard was almost gone, my neck and
    face got sore.
And yet, not sore, in such a sense that any one can see,
But very tender to the touch, and smarted constantly.
I can not think, in lookin' back, what made me quite
    so dumb,
As not to sniff the danger till the worst of it had
    come ;
And yet, a circumstance like that I never knew before,
Where one had lost his whiskers by the overcoat he
    wore.
But that it was the coat alone, is plainly evident ;
Because that only where it touched was where the
    whiskers went.

It must have been the dye-stuff that was used in
    colorin'
The cloth of which the coat was made which had been
    left within ;
A comment on the shiftless way of cleansin' cloth
    that's dyed,
Which ought to make the lazy louts that did it satis-
    fied.
Of course, I've tried most everything that I have read
    about,
But though six months and more have passed I can
    not see a sprout—
Though you may guess I watch for them—that looks
    at all as though
My pepper-sauce and other things was like to make
    them grow.
The only place it didn't touch was just beneath my
    nose,
A little space on both my lips, and there, of course, it
    grows,
And hasn't changed its color, nor it isn't growin' thin,
Like what is left about my face and what is on my
    chin ;
But mustache looks a little odd, with both its corners
    clipped,
As though they wasn't planted right, or somethin'
    had been skipped ;
And so I have to spread them out to cover up the
    space,
And train them, with what skill I can, to occupy the
    place.

And then, because the color holds while all the rest is
    white,
It makes me look so singular in most of people's
    sight ;
And almost all who knew me when my whiskers were
    so thick
Are sure to ask, on meetin' me, if I have not been
    sick,
Till, if I was not conscious that I'm feelin' pretty
    well,
Their askin' all these questions might bring on a
    feeble spell.
And lots of people that I've known for years will pass
    me by
Without a recognition, or without their knowin' why ;
And when I call them by their names, will look their
    blank surprise,
And ask me what's the matter with myself, or with
    their eyes.
My sister's husband passed me twice, one day not
    long ago,
And told a friend that I was some one whom he didn't
    know.
And I declare it makes one feel a little kind o' queer
To grow away from all his friends in less than half a
    year ;
And I can fancy now, I think, how Rip Van Winkle
    felt,
Which made his poor old eyes grow dim, and poor old
    heart to melt,

To think the takin' of a nap should sweep the friends
     away
Whom he had known, and who knew him, within (to
     him) a day.
And then it's quite amusin' just to see some people
     stare,
And wonderin', as I suppose, what ails that fellow's
     hair. ·
Of course, I couldn't blame them, for if I was not
     well bred,
I'd very likely do the same, if I was in their stead ;
There's somethin' so inquisitive within the most of us
That what is very singular is apt to strike us thus.
The query of all queries is, what dyes did they employ
Who made the cloth that gave this coat its power to
     destroy ?
For that it was the dye-stuff in the cloth admits no
     doubt,
As only where it touched the beard the whiskers are
     killed out.
But, though it has its comic side, it is not all a jest,
For whiskers, with the joke left out, have value not
     expressed
In any tables that we know, and yet is just as real
As tabulated values, for it's values that we feel.
A fellow said the other day (my whiskers are so thin),
"The wind won't whistle through the beard that's
     growin' on your chin."
And that's what makes it serious : my chin bereft of
     hair

Will let the winds of winter play their antics round it
    bare.
And who that knows the comfort of a beard upon the
    chin
But that will feel some pity for the fix that I am in?
I've grown too old for pride to hold so very much of
    sway,
And don't feel sore upon that score because they've
    gone away ;
But at my age I've reached the stage when comfort
    counts for more
Than all the pride that occupied my mind in days of
    yore ;
And nature's muff was good enough for me to always
    wear,
And so I should, and so I could, if I'd not lost the
    hair.
But there's a grand philosophy which never looks be-
    hind,
To gather up the blessings lost, to cumber up the
    mind,
But takes the blessings that are left, and feeds upon
    them so,
That, even if they seem but small, they're sure to
    grow and grow,
And fill us with contentment, that the things which
    we possessed
Were, after all, for us and ours, the things that were
    the best.
And so I sing this requiem, about half sad and gay,

Over my whiskers, well beloved, but surely gone
      away,
Then turn, with what philosophy I can, again to look
      ahead,
And train my heart to follow in the path my feet
      must tread.

OLD SCHOOL TEMPERANCE.

(Two representative speeches made at a District
Conference of the M. E. Church, giving a solution of
the liquor question.)
We had some temperance speeches at the Conference
      last night,
Whose brilliant scintillations seemed to shed a flood of
      light,
For those who simply follow what the master thinkers
      think,
About the disposition of the awful curse of drink.
It's always been a "muddle" to the ordinary mind
To solve the vexin' problem, and a remedy to find,
For while the awful evil is an easy thing to see,
There are so many theories they can not well agree.

Some talk of "moral suasion" from the platform and
      the press,
And some of higher license, as the way to make it less ;
Some say that mother's teachin's, and the trainin' of
      the schools,

Must teach the children not to be such alcoholic fools ;
But almost all of them agree it never'll do to mix
A question havin' morals in a nation's politics.
Of course there are some "cranky" folks, with sense
      enough to say
That votes would be the surest means to put the curse
      away ;
And they persist in tryin' it, in all this bitter fight,
Not only that they think it best, but that they feel it's
      right.

But we were told last evenin' that the remedy was
      near,
It's application, also, was expounded very clear ;
Of course it sounded novel and evinced a lot of search,
When speakers solemnly announced "it resteth with
      the church."
We wouldn't think of questionin' their great sagacity,
And only ask about the church, the question "Who
      is she?"
We look in all our meetin's, and are greeted with the
      sight,
Both in the Sabbath services, and every week-day
      night—
Of women, girls and women, and with only now and
      then,
Like daisies in a flower-pot, a sprinklin' of men ;
And then we search the records, and discover, to our
      shame,
That even there proportions are essentially the same.

And then these great addresses seem to have an added
    light,
As we can grasp the meanin' which these speakers
    had in sight.
"*The Church :*" we cease to wonder why they call it
    "her" and "she,"
When women form its membership in such majority ;
We cease to wonder, also, that so many relegate
To "her" the many burdens which they either fear
    or hate.
We see the magnanimity with which these men aver
That this responsibility rests mostly upon "her ;"
And "she," dear soul, a woman, with just men
    enough to wear
The honors of the offices which "she" may have to
    spare.

"The Church," without a ballot, held to answer for
    the cause
Of purer legislation and of less unrighteous laws,
While many who are in it, and can vote as well as pray,
Uphold the license policy on each election day !
God bless our noble women, who, when both their
    hands are tied,
For lack of opportunities of which they are denied,
Still bend their backs to burdens which their brothers
    seek to shirk,
And try, amid discouragements, to do the Master's
    work.

These wise men tell their hearers that when parties
    nominate
"A christian man for office he should be their candi-
    date,
"Without regard to party," and we must infer they
    meant
Without regard to principles the parties represent.
Suppose a license party wants to catch the christian
    vote,
They do not make their platform like a promissory note
By pledgin' party fealty to any righteous cause,
Much less for the enactment of some rigid temperance
    laws.

But place in nomination, now and then, a temperance
    man,
Because his christian character will help along their
    plan ;
And then these preachers tell us that the church
    should help them in
To legislate for righteousness against this awful sin.
If they could reason better, it would seem that they
    might see,
That such a course as they advise would prove it's
    fallacy.
A christian man, in office, is a man to represent
The wishes and the principles of those by whom he's
    sent ;
And no one but a Judas would betray the trust im-
    posed,
To which he had assented, till his term of office closed.

For christians to expect it would expect the man to
       lie,
And make himself obnoxious by an act of perfidy,
As we have found too often, and, alas, in many ways,
When such a man is trusted, whose dictation he obeys.
Experience has proven, in repeated cases, why
The thing these preachers recommend is dangerous to
       try ;
For when a party's platform stands for one thing, and
       the "brother"
Who takes the nomination—in his conscience—for an-
       other,
It don't require a prophet, or a prophet's son, to see,
The   platform, not the conscience, will obtain the
       mastery.

For he's the party's servant, and because of that, must
       stand
For whatsoever measures his constituents demand ;
He's not a private citizen, has not the right of choice,
But, in official station, must express the people's voice.
On any other basis, he could never represent
The people, by whose suffrage this officer was sent.
Then what becomes of arguments and sophistries like
       these,
Before the mind of any who believes the things he
       sees ?

We envy not the preacher, in the midst of such a fray,
Who seeks to be a leader, with no better things to say ;

For if the people follow, votin' only for the man,
Without regard to principles, they'll end where they
        began,
So far as reformation goes ; while drinkin', as a vice,
Has gotten more entrenched in law, by takin' their
        advice.
There's not a liquor dealer that can anywhere be found,
But that will tell these preachers that their argument
        is sound ;
The whole fraternity applaud this doctrine, to a man,
The politicians, also, give endorsement to this plan.

But though these preachers, possibly, may think this
        plan is new
(And we would not dispute them, for to them it may
        be true),
Yet others recollect it as a failure most forlorn,
A generation—more or less—before these men were
        born.
When christian men have grace enough to push aside
        the " sop "
The devil shrewdly offers them, this fallacy will stop,
And when the christian voter learns to see what under-
        lies
The feet of party candidates, 'twill open many eyes.

A christian never need expect, and ought not to desire,
That any party candidate will prove himself a liar.
A man who runs for office—if he's even half a man—
Will stand by his constituents, and help them what
        he can ;

And christians stultify themselves, by hopin', if they
      do,
That any party's candidate will prove himself untrue.
The platforms, not the characters of candidates denote,
Beyond a par adventure, how an officer will vote.

On any other basis we should always be at sea,
And offer costly premiums for party treachery.
Whoever votes for "christians" on a whisky plat-
      form plank,
When they are disappointed, will have just themselves
      to thank.
If conscience is a factor in the officer at all,
He couldn't be expected to obey it's double call ;
Between the voice from Heaven, and the pledges from
      below,
It wouldn't even take a guess to tell which way he'll
      go.
Be done with all this nonsense, and let reason have
      it's sway,
And *vote* for *men* and *measures* that will sweep this
      curse away.

UNCLE ALVIN'S TRIP TO KANSAS.

'Twas just about the holidays of eighteen ninety-four,
When times were pinchin' harder than they'd ever
    done before,
And almost everybody felt that weatherin' the gale
Depended very largely on how close they reefed their
    sail,
And then as much depended on how soon it would
    subside
As on the helmsman's steady hand, how long the craft
    would ride,
That we received a letter from our only brother's wife,
That he, the husband, balanced on the ragged edge of
    life,
With chances so against him that his doctors were in
    doubt
Whether his constitution and their skill could pull
    him out.
He'd been a-failin' all the fall, but since he took his
    bed
He had declined more rapidly, her anxious letter said,
And though they were not certain, his physicians had
    a fear
That his disease was cancer, and if so his end was
    near.
I did some anxious thinkin' for a day or two from that,
For all our family were gone but me and brother Gat,

And he was such a brother, with a heart as brave and
	true
As He, the father of us all, has put in but a few ;
And I was more than conscious that if I was lyin' sick,
With little hope of livin', he would hasten to me quick.
Indeed, I well remembered when our only sister died,
How he had left his business and had hastened to her
	side.
One day my letter reached him with the news that
	she must die,
The next and he was comin' just as fast as cars could
	fly ;
And loyally he waited at her bedside night and day,
The little time she lingered till her spirit left its clay;
And then we stood together where the " dust to dust"
	was said,
And saw her body laid to rest within its narrow bed ;
And when it all was over, I had seen him on the train
To hasten to the duties of his western home again.
Ten years and more of changes were between that
	time and now,
And his dear wife had written me that he was very
	low,
And facin' such conditions how could any one be
	slow
In reachin' the conclusion that his duty was to go ?
And so the thing was settled between me and Nancy
	Jane
That I would spend two weeks away, and she was to
	remain

And 'tend to business, her's and mine, and keep it
     goin' round,
For I knew she could manage so things wouldn't run
     aground.
The first thing was the money, which we know not
     how to spare
For takin' such a journey, to be swallowed up in fare ;
But when we set about it we succeeded in a day
In gettin' what was needed, so that that was out the
     way ;
And while I got my business in the best shape that I
     could,
She spent the day preparin' for my basket somethin'
     good ;
And this was on a Saturday, with ticket bought be-
     side,
And Sunday, after midnight, I must start upon my
     ride.
That Sabbath—none were like it in the more than
     twenty years
That we had shared together in each other's hopes and
     fears—
Was spent about as usual, as far as forms could go,
But in the secret chambers of our hearts it wasn't so.
I was to go at midnight, and she was to stay behind,
With all the unknown future as a blank before the
     mind.
We'd neither of us traveled much, and 'twasn't strange
     that she
(Of course I didn't share it !) felt a little nervously.

We went to church, as common, in the mornin' and
      at night,
And found each service helpful, if our hearts were
      not as light
As they were on occasions when no specter seemed to
      rise
To flaunt his gaudy banner of suggestion in our eyes,
Of what might happen to us in the days to intervene,
With half a continent so soon a-stretchin' in between.
After the evenin' service we, of course, did not retire,
But visited till midnight, sittin' round the winter fire,
Till I had only time to lunch (we called it breakfast).
      Well !
Perhaps the way we parted she would thank me not
      to tell,
And so I won't betray her ; but it may suffice to say
That when her tears had started they were bravely
      brushed away,
And with a kiss and hand-shake our good-byes were
      quickly said,
When I set out for Kansas and my wife set out for
      bed.
I took the "Old Reliable," as Erie folks would say,
And found the midnight train on time, and soon was
      under way.
The coaches were not crowded, and I saw each pas-
      senger
Had, somehow, had two seats apiece assigned to him
      or her,
And still a lot were empty, more than I could occupy,
However much I spread myself, provided I should try.

I simply did as others had, and improvised a bed,
By takin' one seat for my feet, another for my head,
And by a little feignin' sleep by shuttin' up my eyes,
The goddess came along herself and took me by sur-
  prise,
And wooed me off so gently by the rumble and the
  sway
That I was soon unconscious how the engine sped
  away,
And scarcely noticed anything but now and then a
  scream,
Or when the sway and rumble ceased by shuttin' off
  the steam,
Till some time after daylight, when the cars began to
  fill,
By makin' halts for passengers at every little ville,
And we were rudely jostled from our slumber to the
  need
Of makin' room for others, and of course we gave it
  heed,
And 'woke to find the passengers were mostly on their
  way
To Youngstown, in Ohio, for the labor of the day,
And most of them had dinner-pails and dressed to
  indicate
That they were bone and sinew of society and state,
And all got off together at the Youngstown station
  stop,
And hurried, men and women, to their factory or shop.
Of course, it took a little while for us to realize
That we were in Ohio, and recover our surprise ;

And then about the next thing was to conjure up a
          way
To put a little pleasure in a long and weary day,
By givin' mind and body somethin' else to occupy
Than just the simple killin' of the moments as they
          fly ;
So I got out my writin' stuff, with which I was sup-
          plied,
And wrote of things and places which I passed along
          the ride—
A sort o' flyin' journal ; and the plan worked so com-
          plete
That it was almost noon, or quite, before I cared to
          eat ;
And after lunch was finished (what reminder did it
          prove
Of Nancy's sterling common sense as well as thought-
          ful love,
By puttin' in the basket what would tempt my appe-
          tite,
And in such nice arrangement as to be a real delight ;
And it is worth a journey of a day or so to find
One's own appreciation comin' clearer to the mind,
Of every-day devotion, in the common things of life,
Which come without obtrusion from the loving heart
          of wife,
Which don't find recognition in the ordinary way,
While bein' so together in the life of every day),
I laid aside my tablet for a little needed rest,
And studied for a certain time how I could get it best.

I'd always been so active that to ride for half a day,
Without once walkin' up a hill to give the muscles
        play,
Was weariness indeed to me, and I got desperate,
And planned to get some exercise at almost any rate.
So when the whistle sounded, and the train began to
        slow,
I buttoned up my overcoat and gathered up to go,
And struck the depot platform by the time the train
        was still,
And paced it back and forward with more energy
        than skill,
But didn't get so far away that when the "captain"
        roared
His orders for the train to move that I could get aboard.
And so I spent the afternoon, and struck another man,
From way beyond Chicago who was followin' my
        plan,
And then we tramped together when we could, and
        after that,
We spent the moments pleasantly, engaged in friendly
        chat.
He and his wife had visited in "York State" as they
        say,
And now were lookin' westward, and were on their
        homeward way.
I'd finished up my journal-like epistle on the rail,
To drop, as I had promised, in Chicago's evenin' mail,
Addressed, of course, to Nancy Jane, and now that
        we were there,

I found before my other train but half an hour to
    spare ;
And when I'd mailed my letter, as I did upon the
    train,
And got myself unloaded, and was loaded up again,
I hadn't many minutes left to make a swift survey
Of things that were about me till the engine steamed
    away.
We left the "windy city" just a little after eight,
By train whose destination was the sunny golden
    state.
The train was mostly "sleepers," which was equally
    as true
Of coaches as of all on board, except, perhaps, the
    crew.
The screamin' of the whistle and the swayin' of the
    train
Was royal soothin' syrup for the weary flesh and brain,
While floatin' just above us was a sort of comet's tail,
From out the engine's bosom, as we rode upon the
    rail.
The only little episode which any of us met,
Was just behind the writer, on our way to Joliet.
Some "swipes" had got among us, and at once their
    arts applied.
An old man just behind us was the party whom they
    tried ;
They met, as if by accident, beside the old man's
    chair ;
One asked to have a bill exchanged, to pay his sleepin'
    fare.

Of course, the other couldn't, but to work his little
    plan,
He modestly suggested that "perhaps our friend here
    can."
The old man didn't do it, which was just a little
    mean,
But proved that he had lived too long to be accounted
    "green;"
He didn't change the bill for them, but sternly
    answered "nay,"
When asked "if he would kindly tell my friend the
    time of day?"
They loitered round without a seat until the train
    should stop,
And when it did, at Joliet, the trio took a drop.
And on we sped, and on we slept as soundly as we
    might,
The snorin' blendin' nicely with the music of the
    night;
And when the daylight struck us we had ridden
    through a state,
And partly through another, goin' toward the golden
    gate.
But nothin' further happened out of which to weave a
    tale,
But just the din and rattle of a night upon the rail.
The mornin' sky was leaden, and it needed not a seer
To make a person conscious that a winter's storm was
    near.
I got my first impression then, as it would seem to me,
Of bein' on a vessel in the middle of the sea,

With just the little difference of sailin' on a train,
Instead of plowin' out our course across the trackless
     main ;
But east or west, or anywhere we chose to turn our eye,
They only ran a little way before they hit the sky,
And all the earth seemed narrowed up within a little
     space
Which we could cross within an hour, and not increase
     our pace.
I'd always lived among the hills that ridge the Em-
     pire State
In undulations just as far as sight can penetrate,
And still give no impression that the rim was very
     near,
Where anyone could, if he wished, step off the hemi-
     sphere ;
But here, the level prairies have a sense of narrowness,
As difficult to analyze as it was to repress.
It might have been the atmosphere, for anything I
     knew,
So laden with the comin' storm that sight could not
     go through,
Save only for a little space, but be it as it may,
I couldn't outline how it seemed in any other way.
I said a storm was gatherin', of course I didn't know,
By any indication, whether it was rain or snow.
The weather, since I started, up till now, was very
     fine,
With not a bit of snow or ice in sight along the line,
And almost warm enough to ride without a fire by day ;

The nights, of course, were frosty, when the steam-
     pipes came in play.
But presently we noticed that the ice began to form
On water by the roadside and it soon began to storm ;
At first it was as fine as frost, and filtered through the
     air
Almost unnoticed only by the white streaks here and
     there
Upon the little ice-fields in the ditches by the way,
And we were in a blizzard by the middle of the day.
I'd often read about them, but it's quite another thing
To ride into one quickly, from an atmosphere of spring.
We got to Kansas City just about an hour late,
With blizzard ragin' fiercely, and had half an hour to
     wait.
It wasn't quite a picnic for the few of us who must,
To gather up our luggage, and go through the clouds
     of "dust"
Which sifted all about us, and get on another train,
And get ourselves adjusted by the time it moved again ;
Especially the walkin', and the waitin' in the snow,
With mercury at zero, and a quite a way below,
And overshoes within our grip, because we chanced
     to lack,
Just when we might have used it, but a moment to un-
     pack.
(The truth is, we expected that no change would be
     required,
Until we reached the station where our ticket had ex-
     pired,

And that was quite a distance, but the porter made it
      plain,
Without extended argument that we must change our
      train.)
While cars were movin' everywhere, and goin' to and
      fro,
And passengers, with grip in hand, were waitin' in the
      snow,
And frost was creepin' through their cloths to every
      nerve and vein,
Of those of us who waited for the makin' of the train.
But thirty minutes crept around, in spite of frost and
      snow,
And we were told to "get aboard," and soon were on
      the go.
The cars from Kansas City on were sparsely occupied,
And didn't have the heatin' pipes along on either side.
The country we were traversin' had interest to me,
Because of what had happened in it's early history.
My youthful blood was greatly stirred, in those his-
      toric times,
While readin' of the cruel deeds and border-ruffian
      crimes,
Through which the Kansas pioneers had fought their
      bloody way
To statehood and to freedom that she occupies today,
I had a lot of school-day friends who mingled in that
      strife,
And some sealed their devotion by the sacrifice of life.
One noble fellow gave his life, as I remember well,

Within the streets of Lawrence, where so many others
    fell
By the relentless bullets of the ruffians who obeyed
The orders of their chieftain, in the famous Quantrel
    raid.
I loved him as my tutor, when he taught my boyish
    pen,
And later when he ranked among the brainiest of men.
He always stood among the best, with courage to defy
The foes of human freedom, and with fortitude to die.
I wanted to see Lawrence, where his martyr blood was
    shed,
And mingled with the others of her hero patriot dead ;
But though it was in daylight, and we made a mo-
    ment's halt,
The privilege I coveted went by me in default
Of courage that was equal to defy a blizzard's face
To catch some little glimpses, through the storm, of
    such a place ;
And so we passed it thinkin' of the part which had
    been played
Upon the very spot where now the iron rails were
    laid,
Which bore us on so smoothly through the rage of
    such a day,
And paid our grateful homage to the heroes passed
    away.
The storm kept on increasin', and our progress was
    delayed
From keepin' up to schedule time, till I was much
    afraid

That we should reach Emporia, where I must leave the
    main,
And go upon the southern branch, too late to catch the
    train.
Thus far I had been fortunate, and only been delayed
A half hour each at stations where my changes had
    been made ;
But when at seven-thirty, when we reached Emporia,
I found, upon inquiry, that I had a night to stay,
It wasn't a condition, it may easily be guessed,
Though after such a weary ride, invitin' me to rest.
The errand which had brought me there was one re-
    quirin' haste,
And now eleven hours to wait seemed quite a time to
    waste ;
But there was nothin' else to do, as far as I could see,
Than just to make a virtue of a stern necessity.
The storm had ceased by this time, and the stars were
    shinin' clear,
The wind had stopped it's ragin', but the cold was
    most severe.
I found a hotel porter from an inn across the street,
And toward it's hospitality turned my reluctant feet.
The mornin' crisp but pleasant came, and I was up
    and dressed,
Refreshed somewhat by slumber, it must also be con-
    fessed,
And soon was rollin' southward to complete my out-
    ward trip,
With questions runnin' through my thoughts, if not
    upon my lip,

Of whether I should be in time to reach my brother's
    bed,
With him alive to greet me, or should only find him
    dead.
I found on board some passengers who knew my
    brother well,
And one of them, a lawyer, had some pleasant news
    to tell.
He told me he was better ; that he heard the day be-
    fore
That he was able to sit up for half an hour or more,
And that the indications were, as near as they could
    tell,
He might survive for quite a while, and possibly get
    well.
He said that just three days before his symptoms took
    a turn,
With hope almost abandoned, and from what could be
    discerned,
Not owin' to the treatment ; and I think my face be-
    trayed,
If he was half a reader, what relief his words con-
    veyed.
I know I felt like sayin', though I did not speak the
    word,
Yet might been pardoned if I had, a hearty "praise
    the Lord."
I'd sent a card ahead of me the Saturday before,
To tell them I was comin', and their team was at the
    door

When we pulled in the station, and the first one that I
  hit,
After I reached the platform with my little travelin'
  kit,
Was one as tall as I am, who at once began to laugh,
For I looked so exactly like my latest photograph
Which I had sent six months before, he couldn't have
  a doubt
But I was just the passenger that he was lookin' out,
And called me Uncle Al at once, and gave my hand a
  shake,
A little like the Methodists ; not quite enough to
  break
The bones within the fingers, but enough to make one
  sure
That 'tisn't putty they have got, though what they
  can endure.
We had but just a mile or so to ride, but I declare,
I thought my hands would surely freeze before we
  could get there.
I had a pair of common gloves, a little snug, 'tis true,
Of leather (rat-skin kid, I guess) and cotton lined all
  through ;
And when I pulled them on my hands, I thought I
  could defy
The zero weather for a while, and wouldn't need to
  try ;
But when I reached my brother's and had greeted one
  by one,
Of those who formed his household, they were achin',
  oh, like fun ;

And when I had removed my gloves, my bran new
    gloves of kid,
I threw them in a corner, and the first thing that I did
Was plunge my hands in water which I asked my
    niece to bring,
As cold as water could be, and I found it just the thing ;
It wasn't half a minute till the ache began to go,
And left no trace of frost behind either to feel or show.
I found my brother better, though not able yet to
    walk,
But so improved in strength that he could lie in bed
    and talk.
I know I can not hope to make some other person see
Just what that first day's visit was to brother and to me.
We hadn't seen each other for the last ten years or so,
And it can not be wondered that his mouth was bound
    to go ;
He thought of questions faster than a petifogger could,
And put them in a manner that he made them under-
    stood,
Of people and of places that he'd known in years gone
    by,
And kept me—like a witness on the stand to testify—
So busy with my answers that the moments fairly
    flew,
And sometimes I turned questioner to see how much
    he knew,
Till I began to worry, as they came and went so thick,
For fear he'd over-do it and would make himself more
    sick ;

But caution didn't count for much, his tongue ran on
  the same
Without an intermission till the evenin' shadows came,
And even on till ten o'clock beside the winter fire,
Till I, in pity for him, felt it duty to retire.
I can't go into details of the days which followed that,
But one can well conjecture they were pretty full of
  chat.
I told them at the outset of the limit to my stay,
That I had only just two weeks that I could be away ;
And minutes had a value seldom realized before,
With neither of us knowin' what the future held in
  store.
His children were all married, and were settled near
  at hand,
The boys all bein' farmers, owning each a piece of
  land
From one to four miles out from home, and I must
  spend a day
To visit at the home of each before I came away,
A thing, of course, that I enjoyed, and only could re-
  gret
That it could not be longer by the limits I had set.
They had revival meetin's at the village every night,
About a mile from brother's, though a little out of
  sight,
Because a belt of timber and some orchards lay be-
  tween,
But otherwise the village and the church could have
  been seen.

'The children went each evenin', and of course invited
    me,
And I went partly, I confess, of curiosity ;
Not that revival meetin's did not have an interest,
Without another motive to attend them in the West,
For I had come from one at home, and witnessed with
    delight,
The people turnin' to the Lord by dozens every night ;
But I was anxious to attend so far from home to see,
If they had better methods of conductin' them than we.
I took a lively interest, and took along some fire
To help along the meetin', if occasion should require.
The house was filled with people, and they mostly
    seemed to pay
Attention to the preacher and hear what he had to say ;
But when the sermon ended with a logical appeal,
There wasn't in it anything to make the people feel,
And scarcely anybody moved, but stood with one ac-
    cord,
As though they had no interest in turnin' to the Lord.
I couldn't help but wonder if the ministry were sent
To win the world to Jesus by cold-blooded argument.
I felt the gospel fever to my very finger-tips,
And, later in the meetin' it came out between my lips,
At first around the altar, for a single soul was there,
And members were not over free to lift their voice in
    prayer ;
And when the preacher afterward gave opportunity
For those of us who loved the Lord to briefly testify,
I couldn't help but tell them, in an earnest, tender
    word,

That I had found a blessin' in the service of the Lord.
Four nights I went to meetin', which was all that I
    could spare
Away from brother's bed-side, of the time I could be
    there.
Not over half a dozen had, as far as I could see,
Accepted of salvation with the opportunity.
It always makes me sad to see that men can ever seem
To lack an inspiration when they handle such a theme,
And follow out their argument as stoical as though
It simply meant a business deal, instead of endless woe.
I can not comprehend it, how a man whom God has
    sent
To preach the blessed word of life can be at all con-
    tent,
By goin' through the formula from week to week and
    not
Expect and plan for victory, and do it on the spot.
This goin' through the sacred forms in regular routine,
Without expectin' fruitage, is too much like a ma-
    chine ;
And preachers needn't wonder, and they ought not to
    inquire
Why multitudes are so unreached, till they shall get
    on fire,
And preach a red-hot gospel, which can reach the
    uttermost,
And make the sinner tremble, and completely save the
    lost.
I'd call it a misfortune if they had the multitudes
To listen to their arguments, so much like platitudes,

While they were unconverted, for they naturally
  would grow
More callous to the gospel claims the longer they
  should go.
And sinners are not all to blame, who listen year by
  year,
To preachers who are not enthused, and seldom shed
  a tear,
Or manifest a grave concern for fear they may be lost,
Nor strive to win them to the Lord at almost any cost,
But preach their sermons, two by two, as Sabbaths
  come and go,
And ask no further questions whether men will yield
  or no.
The preachers are a brainy lot, when taken as a class,
But if we were to judge them by the things they bring
  to pass,
They would not measure, even up, with those who
  drive the plow,
Or teach, or get their livin' by their labors anyhow.
The preacher's livin' is assured (a sort of favored lot)
If he goes through the motions, whether he succeeds
  or not,
While competition forces almost every other class
To figure their successes by what they can bring to
  pass.
The fault is in their methods, for they overlook, some-
  how,
That even worldly men succeed by seizin' on the *now*,
While that old gospel which they preach proclaims no
  other way

Than just to offer and accept the gospel hope " to-day."
Yet weeks and months and years go by, in some men's
    ministry,
Without an invitation for convicted souls to try
The virtue of the gospel plan, by openin' the way
For them to do it on the spot, and make no more de-
    lay.
The "now" was meant for preachers quite as much,
    and may be more,
To seize their opportunities, as those they stand be-
    fore,
And wisely cast the gospel net, as they who fish for
    men,
While they were interested, and to do it there and
    then.
If I have got a steer for sale, I don't think I would say
To any interested man " please call another day,"
I'd try and close the deal at once ; and every business
    man,
Who is at all successful always follows such a plan.
If winnin' souls is business, who is dull enough to say
That it will not succeed the best by such a business
    way ?
And I have seen the method tried and prove a grand
    success,
In leadin' many souls from sin to lives of righteous-
    ness,
By makin' text and sermon keep this single end in
    view,
Then shake the tree and gather fruit as soon as it is
    through.

What sort of an evangelist would any preacher be
Who carried out the methods of the common ministry ;
Who gave a Bible lecture full of argument to prove
That God has sent His only Son, to manifest His love,
And open up a fountain, as a remedy for sin,
And gave no invitation for the people to plunge in?
And if the open fountain needs an always open door,
To make it most effectual and gather in the more,
Then why should preachers follow in an antiquated
        rut,
And keep the door of privilege effectually shut?
If souls are what they're preachin' for, their measure
        of success
Is measured by the number which their labors reach
        and bless,
And he who wins no trophies for his Lord—it seems
        to me—
May doubt his methods, or his call to such a ministry.
Why shouldn't every service have enough of Pentecost
To fire the heart of preachers with a zeal to save the
        lost,
And bring the open fountain just as near the sinner's
        feet
As privilege can do it, and as often as they meet?
I've wondered, as I've witnessed such a lack of busi-
        ness sense,
How men can lay their failures of success to Provi-
        dence,
When even children manifest, in all their little games,
No expectation of results above their childish aims.

The one thing to be prayed for most devoutly, I should
 say,
Is that the fire of God may fall, and quickly burn away
The notion from the thoughts of men, in pulpit and
 in pew,
That God intends His harvests to be gathered by the
 few.
The question of "the multitudes" which occupy the
 pen
Of many of our ministers and literary men,
And how to reach and save them by the gospel's
 gentle power,
Is one whose quick solution is more needful every
 hour ;
But preachin' will not do it, in the ordinary way,
Nor prayers accomplish very much, as most of people
 pray.
But when the preachers are baptised with love for
 dying men,
Which takes the gospel to them with their lips, and
 not their pen,
And goes himself, and leads his flock to do those help-
 ful deeds
Which manifests a sympathy with other people's
 needs,
And teaches the sweet gospel of our common brotherhood,
The church will reach the multitudes, and do a lot of
 good.
The church could get a lot of hints of how to win
 success,

By thinkin' of her duty more, and human weakness
    less,
And watchin' how the enemies they battle operate ;
They never think of weakness, and they never sit and
    wait
For people to come to them, and don't call it sacrifice
To do some inconvenient things without regard to
    price ;
But go about the business in a business sort of way,
A lot more anxious to succeed than they are for to
    pay.
A sort of inspiration takes possession of the mind,
To spread their vile infection to the others of their
    kind,
And makes them swift and skillful to inoculate their
    kin,
With all the hateful virus of the leprosy of sin.
And christians ought to learn of them, and might if
    they were shrewd,
The way the gospel may be made to reach the multi-
    tude.
They might, with profit, copy from their hand to hand
    appeal,
And show the same "abandon" in the matter of their
    zeal,
With equal consecration, in the work which they en-
    gage,
And have an equal courage in the warfare which they
    wage.
Indeed, we ought to shame them, by exceedin' them
    in zeal,

As much as heavenly joys exceed the pleasures which
    they feel ;
As much as our commission is above the one they bear,
By leadin' men to Heaven, while they lead them to
    despair ;
As much as inspiration by the Holy Ghost imparts
A mightier upliftin' to our human minds and hearts,
Than any one that can come to them from any source
    they know ;
And yet their feet are often swift, while christians feet
    are slow.
I'd like to know if every one, when Christ comes in
    the heart,
Is not, by that relation, as completely set apart
To help Him spread His kingdom till the last man
    shall be won,   .
As by the layin' on of hands—by whomsoever done ?
Each man and woman of us, of whatever name or creed,
Hold just as high commission, if we have the sense to
    read,
As any that can come to men, to make our efforts tell,
Up to their utmost limit, in redeemin' men from hell.
The fact that we don't know it—as is evidently true
Of many who are christian in the forms which they go
    through—
Proves either our stolidity, or serves to indicate,
As sure as a thermometer, what is our inward state.
God send his blessin' on us, in the pulpit and the pew,
To give us comprehension of the work we need to do,
And wisdom as to methods, lest we make the grave
    mistake,

Of callin' motion progress, in the efforts that we make ;
But not the kind of blessin' for which most of
    christians sigh,
Which simply means a feelin' of an inward ecstacy,
That spends itself in shoutin' more than efforts made
    to win
The lost who are about them from the fatal power of
    sin.
We need that kind of blessin' which will make us ap-
    prehend
What means will most contribute to the most desired
    end,
And then imparts the courage for it oftener than not,
To follow where the Spirit leads, will call for quite a
    lot ;
A blessin' too, that gives us the ability to see
That our success will not depend on brains and
    brilliancy,
So much as on the Spirit's help, in efforts made to win
The lost who are about us from the awful power of sin.
The Spirit ! ah, the Spirit of the Master which can
    go
To any heights above us, or to any depths below,
To reach and win a single soul, and not a thought
    arise,
In all our seekin' after them, that it was sacrifice !
But we shall be impelled by love, to do the best we
    can,
To take the great salvation to another fellow man,
Because it has embraced him, in the great provision
    made,

And on the same conditions as ourselves, and needs
      our aid ;
Because he stands beside us in a common brother-
      hood,
With equal possibilities for gettin' equal good ;
Exposed to equal peril from the thunderbolts of wrath
Which fall, in simple justice, upon every sinner's
      path ;
With us, when mercy found us, and received us to a
      place
Among the hosts of others, in the kingdom of His
      grace.
Well, time is never swifter than it is when we would
      stay,
The flyin' minutes, if we could, provokin' some delay ;
And so I found the limit to my visit drawin' nigh,
When I must journey homeward, and must bid my
      friends good-bye,
For just how long a period I couldn't help but see
Was shrouded in the mazes of a great uncertainty.
That brother was improvin' at a rate which justified
Our hopes of his recovery could not be well denied ;
He visited incessantly without fatigue or harm,
And felt no little wish, of course, to show me 'round
      the farm,
While I was more than satisfied to see him on the gain,
And let the boys conduct me through the ancestral
      domain.
I didn't wonder that he felt a little thrill of pride
At ownin' such a prairie farm and timber belt beside ;

He had some twenty acres of as fine a timber belt
As one could well imagine, lyin' west of where he
    dwelt,
Which served the double purpose of a wind-brake
    from the storm,
And fuel for his kitchen and to keep his household
    warm.
And then such level acres of a soil so rich and deep,
Where nature's hidden treasures have been stored
    away to keep
For generations yet unborn, but dolin' to the need,
At each succeedin' harvest, of the mouths that she
    must feed,
With resource undiminished, if we measure by the
    yield
Of yearly golden harvests that are gathered from the
    field.
The last days of my visit he was able to be dressed,
And sit in his accustomed place at table with the rest,
And tried his hand at walkin', for a little, with a cane,
The afternoon I came away, out doors and back again.
The children came to see me off, and when they all
    were there,
My brother's wife requested me to lead them all in
    prayer ;
And so we knelt together, for the last time, as it proved,
Commendin' everything to God concernin' those we
    loved ;
Then took a hasty supper, and amid their tearful eyes,
Gave each of them a partin' hand, and said the sad
    good-byes,

And started for the station ; and, of course, I needn't
     say
I did some solemn thinkin' while we slowly rode
     away.
The train was due at six o'clock and this was Thurs-
     day night,
And if we had no accidents, and made connections
     right,
I planned that I should be at home, twelve hundred
     miles away,
A little in the evenin' of the comin' Saturday,
But when I reached Emporia, and struck the Santa Fe,
At nine o'clock that evenin', it was plain enough to
     see
My plans were disconcerted by the men who operate
The train that was to bring me, for I had five hours
     to wait.
I waited at a hotel just across the street instead
Of stayin' at the station, but I didn't go to bed.
I had an opportunity of seein', all unsought,
The strength of Prohibition in a way I had not
     thought ;
I'd heard so many tellin' of its failures where 'twas
     tried,
And had my own opinions that they didn't know, or
     lied,
Because I knew enough of law to know that, any-
     where,
The people could enforce it if they wanted to, or dare,
And if a law is broken down, it only goes to show,

That men are either cowards, or so vile they want it
     so ;
For here in free America manhood is stultified
When such a declaration shall be anywhere denied,
And arguments are needless, and a waste of time and
     pains,
To prove a thing so evident to anyone with brains.
A man came in the hotel who had been to see a play
That educates the people in a modern sort of way,
By actin' out before them, till it seems reality,
Some case of love's betrayal, or of lust and tragedy,
That evenin', at the theater; a man whose breath be-
     trayed
That he was in the secret of the "boot-leg" whiskey
     trade,
While in the outside pocket of his overcoat I saw
A silent, black-nosed witness to an outraged, broken
     law ;
And presently the night-clerk had arisen from his seat,
And crossed the room to where he stood, and stumped
     him for a treat.
Without a word, he passed it out, but looked a little
     queer,
As if he half suspected that some spotters might be
     near ;
The night-clerk tipped the bottle with a relish, one
     could see,
And when his thirst was satisfied, he proffered it to me.
Politely I declined it, and received for a reply,
"I took you for a Prohi," but he didn't tell me why,
And by the way he said it, it was not quite evident

Whether it was intended as a slur or compliment.

He handed back the bottle, which would hold a quart
  or more,

And it was carelessly replaced where it had been before.

The stranger was a spare-built man, whose looks
  would indicate

The "cow-boy" type of citizen, from some uncertain
  State,

And yet he was good-lookin', with an eye as black as
  night,

With hair and beard to match them, while his hands
  were soft and white ;

His wide-rim hat became him, and he had that easy
  air,

In both his dress and manners, of a man that doesn't
  care ;

As far removed from sloven as he was from common
  dude,

And reticent as one could be, without appearin' rude ;

He only spoke when spoken to, and then in curt reply,

So different from most of men when they are on the
  " fly ; "

And all the information which the night-clerk seemed
  to gain

Was that, like me, he waited for the early mornin'
  train.

He said, when asked the question if he wanted to retire,

That he would take his lodgin' in the chair beside the
    fire ;
And suitin' action to the word, he slid down in a chair,
With feet upon the table, and was soon a snorin'
    there.
With crazy whiskey in him, and a cozy fire outside,
He couldn't well have kept awake, provided he had
    tried.
The clerk and I kept chattin', while I waited for the
    train,
Partly for information of the place which I could gain,
By plyin' him with questions of a character to draw
What he knew of the failure of the Prohibition law.
The city had twelve thousand, and he said that one
    could find,
Provided they were hunters, a few " tigers " that were
    " blind,"
Where whiskey of the vilest sort was sold upon the
    sly,
And mostly by the " demi-monde," to those who wish
    to buy,
But nowhere that he ever knew could open bars be
    seen,
With nothin' more to hide them than the ordinary
    screen.
Our sleeper with the bottle had a quiet nap awhile,
His head thrown back against the wall, his feet upon
    the stile,
Or on the office table ; but it soon was evident
His stomach wasn't sharin' in the general content.

He twitched, and flung his feet about, from table to
the floor,
Without an interruption in the volume of his snore,
And presently we noticed that his bosom rose and fell,
And yielded to the pressure of a mighty upward swell,
Which sent a jet of fluids in a skyward, fragrant spray,
Which fell back in his bosom, and baptized him
where he lay.
The night clerk tried to wake him, or at least to turn
him o'er,
To spare his clothes, and let the spray upon the office
floor ;
But he resisted stoutly, and between a growl and
groan,
Demanded, in no modest terms, that he be let alone.
The clerk was glad to turn away, and let him slumber
on,
For such another picture, we presume, was never
drawn.
He got his whisky slyly, but the picture that we saw
Was quite a vindication of defied and broken law.
His clothes would be a witness which no court could
set aside,
If he should be arraigned before the law he had defied.
I hoped the object-lesson might, perhaps, assist the
clerk
To shun the whisky devil, when he saw his fearful
work ;
But didn't feel like askin', as between his company,
Which one he had enjoyed the most, his drunken
chum or me.

I might be " Prohibition," but it couldn't well be
    said,
That ever, in its practice, I had wholly lost my head,
Or spoiled my clothes with vomit, or disgusted com-
    pany
With such an exhibition as was sickenin' to see.
The train pulled in at two a. m., and while the sleeper
    lay
As drunk and sleepy as before, I quickly rode away.
I don't rejoice when anyone has met discomfiture,
Which brings an added burden for a fellow to endure ;
But when we left without him, it was not with much
    regret
To leave the most disgustin' sight my eyes had ever
    met.
I'd seen a thousand drunkards, and in almost every
    stage,
From beardless boys of tender years to men of hoary
    age,
And heard their drunken jabber, when their tongues
    were gettin' thick,
Recitin' smutty stories that would make a buzzard
    sick ;
Had seen the sidewalks covered with the drunkard's
    filthy spew,
In almost every license place that I had traveled
    through ;
But "boot-leg" whisky takes the palm, of things I
    ever saw,
To be it's own detective for a violated law.

We got to Kansas City, where by traveler's common
    fate,
We found, upon inquiring, we had two more hours to
    wait.
The mornin' sky was cloudy, and the piercin' winter
    breeze
Would chill one to the marrow, though the water
    didn't freeze.
I didn't leave the station far, for keepin' near a fire
Had more than curiosity to satisfy desire.
At nine the train was ready, but we hadn't traveled
    long
Before I found regretfully that I had figured wrong ;
We stopped at every station, and were makin' head-
    way slow,
When I had but the one desire that they would let her
    go.
But presently the sun came out, and such a perfect
    day
Could hardly have been equaled in the very heart of
    May.
We rode with windows open through a landscape
    which to see
Would captivate a scion of the art of husbandry.
The broad and level prairies, which were dotted here
    and there
With signs of thrift and culture, and the black soil
    everywhere,
Would make an eastern farmer—if he hadn't lots of
    grace—

Grow almost green with envy at the owners of the
    place.
I felt a compensation for the dronin' speed we made,
In leisurely surveyin' all the beauty there displayed,
And spent the day delightfully, in spite of all my
    haste,
And grudgin' of the moments which our frequent stops
    would waste.
The night was not as pleasant, but I found reclinin'
    chairs
Were better than the rigid seats for droppin' off one's
    cares,
And slept and walked the aisles by turns, and got as
    much repose
As one could be expected to, with corns upon his toes.
The weather took a tumble, from the laughin' lap of
    May,
Before we reached Chicago, to a snow-white winter's
    day,
And overcoats and rubbers were no longer held for
    show,
But rendered grateful service in Chicago's fleece of
    snow.
We reached the Dearborn station, and unloaded from
    the train,
To find a wait of seven hours before we'd start again ;
We took our breakfast leisurely, and for a little toll,
We checked our grip and basket, and then started for
    a stroll.
The first thing we consulted was a large directory,

To locate certain places which we cared the most to
    see,
And then set out to find them, through the grime and
    soot and snow
Which lay about two inches deep on things both high
    and low,
And didn't see a sidewalk in that stroll of half a day,
That showed the slightest evidence of bein' cleaned
    away.
The snow was just about like sand beneath a person's
    feet,
And there was little choice between the sidewalk and
    the street.
I reached the points of interest for which I started out,
With only the directory to indicate the route.
I got in conversation with a man the night before,
Whom I should take for sixty, or perhaps a trifle more,
Who'd spent a month of fruitless search in California,
To find a younger brother, who, he told me went away
Some twenty years or more ago, from whom he
    hadn't heard,
After the first few letters, not a solitary word,
And he set out to find him, and had made the journey
    there,
Out from his home in Canada, and hunted everywhere,
And made inquiry for him through the California
    press,
By askin' any one who knew to send him his address ;
Till he was taken sick himself, and for a week or so
It seemed a little doubtful whether he would live or no ;

And when the tide turned backward he felt fully justi-
fied
To take his journey homeward just as soon as he could
ride,
And yet with great reluctancy, and feelin', as he said,
That such suspense was even worse than knowin' he
was dead.
His story and his feeble health aroused my sympathy,
The more, undoubtedly, because of what had come to
me.
At two o'clock that afternoon I bade a glad adieu
To loungin' in Chicago, and had started out anew,
This time on board an Erie train, a flyer, and I knew
That wouldn't stop at every place that she was passin'
through ;
And somehow, when I took my seat in that familiar
train,
There came a sort of feelin' that I was at home again.
I saw, as we were pullin' out, a cutter and a sleigh,
The first of either I had seen while I had been away ;
In fact, through all the winter, for before I went from
home,
Even the Christmas sleighin' that was wished for
hadn't come.
There were a lot of empty seats, but when I vainly
tried
To open two together, for a little cozier ride,
A brakeman who was passin' through the train po-
litely said,
An order had been issued that the seats were not a
bed.

Of course, I recognized the fact, but hadn't ridden far,
Before I found a double seat, the first one in the car,
And both of them unoccupied, so I had found my
  "bed,"
And hadn't done a single thing that was prohibited.
And when I got myself arranged as restful as I could,
For weariness had not progressed up to the sleepin'
  mood,
I mused upon the company's refusin' to provide,
By such a crumb of comfort, for the passengers who
  ride,
And wondered if that order wasn't born of some in-
  trigue
Between the Pullman and themselves, by joinin' in a
  league,
Whereby to help the Pullman folks to force an extra
  fare
From those who feel they must have rest, and cannot
  get it there.
And yet they may have done it from an overflow of
  pride,
To keep folks in position they consider dignified ;
For people stretched across the seats to sleep, I will
  admit,
Don't cut as fine a figure as the passengers who sit.
But weary nature doesn't care so much for dignity,
That she can sit bolt upright, just for other folks to
  see ;
But when she is prescribed for room is liable to squirm
Into some sad contortions, and to tie up, like a worm.

I do not know exactly where my cogitations stopped,
But somewhere near the middle, I conclude, the shuttle
        dropped ;
For when I woke at midnight there was quiet in the
        room
Where lately it was flyin' through the web of fancy's
        loom ;
And just across the alley from the " bed " I occupied
My wakin' thoughts were startled by a little child that
        cried.
The weary lookin' mother did her best to still the cry,
Which baby's voice was givin' out, without his
        knowin' why,
Except that he was feelin' in a splendid cryin' mood,
And exercised his liberty, and cried because he could.
But if he could have reasoned, he might well felt jus-
        tified
For makin' all those noises, by his long and tiresome
        ride ;
His mother told me later, when the weary eyes were
        closed,
And for a little interval her children both reposed,
That they had traveled all the week, and now were
        on their way
From clear across the continent, where ocean breezes
        play,
To join her husband in the East, near to her child-
        hood home,
Where he had gone some months before, and now
        wished her to come.

They'd started out together, when their hopes were
    beatin' high,
With what they should accomplish in the brilliant bye
    and bye,
As soon as they were married, and had done their level
    best
To carve out that prosperity they sought, by goin'
    West ;
And for a while they flourished, and their dreams
    seemed comin' true,
Because he got good wages, and had lots of work to do ;
But when the panic struck the West, they saw the
    bubble burst,
For laborers were, everywhere, the ones to feel it
    worst,
And he was forced to leave his wife and little ones
    behind,
To seek again their Eastern home, and try what he
    could find ;
And now, as I have stated, she was goin' back to-day,
With just her two sweet children more than what she
    took away.
I hadn't been inquisitive to learn her history,
But what of it she gave me, she did voluntarily,
Moved by those intuitions which lead people to dis-
    close
Some things to utter strangers, of their happiness or
    woes ;
For public lines of travel, where so many strangers
    meet,

And ride for days together, almost touchin' hands and
    feet,
Break down conventionalities, and make partitions
    thin,
Which makes us slow to recognize that all mankind
    are kin.
Sometimes a high-born fellow can maintain his grip,
    and hold
A frigid reservation from the folks of common mold,
And pose among his fellows as a sort of self-crowned
    king,
But they go on without him with but little bothering.
The homage that is given him is difficult to find,
Outside the strange gyrations of his own belittled mind.
There's not a school like travel, which confers such
    high degrees
On those who have the sense to use its opportunities,
Which broadens our conception of the oneness of our
    race,
And links the poles together in such brevity of space.
I fell to musin', as I saw the woman drop her head,
Almost the moment when her babe at last was quieted ;
And sleep from sheer exhaustion, yet with quickened
    sense which heard,
Almost the slightest noises when her sleepin' babies
    stirred ;
And wondered, as I witnessed it, how much I really
    knew
About that sort of weariness that she was passin'
    through ;

I, who had nothin' but my grip that needed any care,
And that might quickly be bestowed it mattered little
    where,
And all the room I needed, and no person to molest,
By needin' my attention, any attitude of rest,
Until I almost felt ashamed for even havin' tried
To find a restful attitude for portions of my ride.
The first time in my history I saw a Sabbath dawn
Through flyin' latticed windows, as our train sped on
    and on.
The stops were so infrequent that a quiet seemed to
    reign,
Peculiar to the Sabbath, even there upon the train ;
A sacred hush, I fancied, took possession of each
    breast,
Through which the mystic presence of the Lord was
    manifest.
We heard no ringin' church-bells at the customary
    time,
Callin' on us to worship by the voice of every chime ;
We heard no pealin' organ, or the voice of any choir,
To furnish inspiration, or give wings to our desire ;
But, somehow, every whistle of the engine seemed to
    say,
And rumblin' wheels responded back, "This is the
    Sabbath day."
At nine o'clock, or thereabout, I saw my lady friend
Gettin' herself in readiness to reach her journey's end,
And when the whistle sounded, and the station hove
    in sight,
She gathered up her babies to be ready to alight,

While I was glad to help her in such manner as I
    could,
By takin' out her luggage, as a fellow traveler should,
And shared, somewhat, her pleasure, in the welcome
    she received,
As well as from the care and strain of which she was
    relieved.
After the train was under way, the balance of my ride
Was made with the conductor seated closely at my
    side.
I'd seen the man converted just before I went away,
And now was more than glad to hear the things he
    had to say.
He kept his Bible with him, and he said, as well he
    might,
That time he spent in readin' it afforded him delight,
And made him feel how rich he was, with such a
    boundless store
To minister to all his needs, now and forever more.
Or course my first inquiry was who had been gathered
    in,
And started for the kingdom, from the slippery paths
    of sin ;
And when he mentioned over names that I had
    known so well,
It thrilled me with a pleasure which no words can fitly
    tell ;
And still the work was goin' on ; that was the best of
    all,
And souls were nightly yieldin' to accept the gospel
    call.

Though ridin' on the Sabbath wasn't just the means
    of grace
That I would have selected, yet He sanctified the
    place,
And made a sacred music from the rumble and the
    roll,
And cars a house of worship, and a bethel to my soul.
And when the brakeman came along and shouted
    "Hornellsville,"
I had my grip and basket by the time the cars were
    still,
And lit out on the platform at a most becomin' gait,
And took the shortest cut for home, though not ex-
    actly straight.
I found, on Monday mornin', when I took it up again,
That business hadn't suffered in the hands of Nancy
    Jane ;
Bein' my only partner, she knew mostly what to do,
And all the time I'd been away, had done the work of
    two.
She felt some disappointment at my gettin' home so
    late,
For twelve or twenty tardy hours seems quite a while
    to wait,
But knew what slight contingencies would disconcert
    a plan,
And kept her head as level as a loyal woman can.
The sequel to my Kansas trip, it may be fair to state,
Was sadder than the reader may, perhaps, anticipate.
The brother for whose sake I went, and who I visited,

And whom I left improvin' so, in four short months
  was dead.
We knew what caused his trouble, for a builder's scaf-
  fold fell,
And strained him somewhere inwardly, but how we
  couldn't tell.
His doctors had a theory, which possibly was so,
But they were frank enough to own they truly didn't
  know—
That cancer had developed from the injury he got,
Yet had some doubts about it whether it was so or not ;
But while he mended for a time, and got so he could
  ride,
And do some little business that would keep him oc-
  cupied,
It soon became apparent that no human skill could
  save,
Or much retard his progress in his journey to the
  grave,
And at an early mornin' hour in the sweet scented
  May,
Surrounded by his family, he calmly passed away.

UNCLE ALVIN ON SUNDAY EXCURSIONS.

I s'pose I'm puritanical, in notions which I hold,
And newer things seem kind o' strange, because I'm
      gettin' old ;
And like enough, by leavin' them to loiter ,in my
      mind,
The world may be a goin' on and leavin me behind.
And if, to younger folks, I seem as goin' rather slow,
I guess it doesn't matter much, I haven't far to go,
And I confess I rather like a little slower pace,
For 'twon't seem quite so sudden when I reach the
      stoppin' place.

But I've been thinkin' if the day the Lord has always
      blessed,
Has in it nothin' more for men than just a day of
      rest ;
And if it's just as well for them to see what they can
      find,
Of any sort of pleasant way to occupy their mind?
If God is God at all, and has a right to have His say,
What right have men, whom He has made, to put His
      thought away,
By spendin' it a huntin' up some pleasant thing to see,
Or, worse than that, by joinin' in some sort of revelry?

I know the railroad companies are so considerate,
In thinkin' of the workin' men, whose burdens are so
    great,
That they (dear souls) will sacrifice half their accus-
    tomed fare,
To let the workman and his folks go almost any-
    where,
On this, the only day they have, as every workman
    feels,
To leave the counter, or the shop, or busy hum of
    wheels ;
And one would think, to read their "ads," that ridin'
    was so cheap
That money they work hard to earn is 'most a sin to
    keep.

Of course, it's all of "sympathy" for these poor
    workin' men,
That cheap excursions are got up on Sundays, now
    and then ;
And I suppose it's "sympathy" which leads them to
    supply
A certain kind of beverage, whenever they get dry ;
And "sympathy" is manifested almost everywhere,
Till, like enough, the fellow spends much more than
    he can spare,
And how he's rested from his toil, at night, when he
    gets home,
And feels refreshed to enter on the week which is to
    come.

And what if conscience whispers up, as possibly it
    might,
And gets to be impertinent, about it's bein' right
For men to take their families, upon the Sabbath day,
And go a-huntin' pleasure in this careless sort of way ?
D'you s'pose it makes a difference with anybody's lot,
Whether the God who made them shall be pleased
    with them or not ?
And ain't it sin to help it on, in any sort, for gain,
As truly as the plannin' it, or runnin' of a train ?

THE CHRISTIAN'S WEATHER GAUGE.

It snowed a little yester-night, the consequences were
That all our city churches had a lot of seats to spare.
The weather wasn't very cold, nor was there any
    " blow,"
And walkin' wasn't difficult through half an inch of
    snow ;
Yet those who were commissioned to proclaim the gos-
    pel news
Were forced to do it mainly to a lot of empty pews.
The few who love the house of God, and joy to share
    His grace,
Were sparsely scattered here and there in their ac-
    customed place.

It wasn't so this mornin' when the week-day's work
    began,
The snow was no obstruction to a single business man ;
And women didn't hesitate, as we could see, to go,
Without a sign of shrinkin' through the half an inch
    of snow.
The shop-girls hastened briskly, and without apparent
    ill,
To counter, desk or factory with seeming cheery will,
And even city shoppin', if a lady wished to go,
Was not considered hazardous, or hindered by the
    snow.

And men, with dinner-pails in hand, or with their
    kits of tools,
Were goin' to their daily toil, and children to the
    schools.
We doubt if anybody thought that any work must
    stop,
Because "the weather-bureau" let some little snow-
    flakes drop.
But, somehow, it was different last evenin', for the
    snow
Was such a dread to christians that they felt they
    need not go,
Because it was the Sabbath, and the work was only
    praise,
And therefore less important than the work of other
    days.

Two standards evidently must obtain in christian's
     creeds,
The one a pleasant sentiment, the other earnest deeds ;
The sentiment pertainin' to the blessed King of Kings,
The earnest work pertainin' to the world of common
     things.
Of course, they couldn't be reversed, for common
     sense would say
That human needs could not be met in such an easy
     way ;
The bread and butter battle is no easy fight to win,
And that's the sort of struggle that the most of us are
     in.

But when it comes to carin' for the christian's higher
     needs,
They do nct hear, the most of them, the call for
     earnest deeds ;
They follow inclinations, and see not how these re-
     veal,
And gauge, to even human eyes, the interest they feel,
For *men* do *what they want to*, as the world has come
     to know,
In spite of little mists of rain, or little falls of snow ;
And empty seats, on Sabbath, have a voice with
     which they say,
In no uncertain language, why the people stayed away.

And so the "gauge" of weather, be it either snow or
     rain,
Is only an occasion that will make their choices plain,

And test their loyalty to God, a test that must be fair,
By standards of their week-day life, in practice every-
    where.
We question, gravely question, whether anything will
    go,
Before the court of Heaven, in the form of rain or
    snow,
As reason for neglectin' any service that we may,
Which wouldn't be an obstacle to week-day work or
    play.

If business is important, which relates to earthly
    needs,
And justifies—in it's pursuit—stern thought and
    earnest deeds,
And laughs at dificulties, and defies the storm we
    meet,
And trips along life's rugged ways with eager, flying
    feet,
What comment on our estimate of what the King of
    Kings
May have in store for human souls among his heavenly
    things,
That our pursuit is hindered, or our feet refuse to go
Along the upward path-way, on account of rain or
    snow.

If feelings, or convenience were the tests that men
    applied
To lines of earthly business, would their needs be
    satisfied ?

Does God accept our "shamin'", and excuses that
    we give,
To cover up the worldly, or the listless lives we live?
It doesn't take a mountain in our path way to reveal
To others—if not to ourselves—the interest we feel
In the Redeemer's kingdom, over there, or here
    below,
The "weather guage" will test it, by a simple fall
    of snow.

UNCLE ALVIN GOES TO HEAR A GREAT SINGER.

I went to hear a singer that had gotten quite a name,
Because I'd heard so many folks a speakin' of her
    fame,
And how delightfully she sang, that I began to feel
That sometime I would hear her sing, if I could make
    the deal ;
And when I saw it advertised what night she would
    appear,
I planned that Nancy Jane and I would also then be
    here,
And get our seats as near the front as cleverly we
    could,
So we could see just how she looked, and hear her
    pretty good.

It cost us half a dollar each, but that I didn't mind
(Though dollars don't lay very thick for workin' folks
       to find),
And we were fortunate enough, because we wasn't
       late,
To get a pair of seats in front, that suited us first-rate ;
And sat there half an hour, or more, while folks were
       gathering,
For lots of other people came, like us, to hear her sing ;
And while I waited for her I kept looking round to
       see
About how many dollars' worth of people there might
       be.

And I should say a thousand, and perhaps a little
       more,
Had bought her reputation which had come along be-
       fore,
Just like ourselves, and if the thing should be but
       second rate,
She'd have our money, anyhow, regrets would come
       too late.
I thought five hundred dollars was quite a little sum,
For just a single one to earn within two hours to come ;
For I have worked a whole year hard, and do it every
       year,
With Nancy's work thrown in beside, and don't make
       that much clear.

And while such worldly thoughts as these were
    troopin' through my mind
The curtain, all at once, rose up, and she stood just
    behind.
And when 'twas run up high enough, she made a
    graceful bow,
And then the audience got wild, I thought, and think
    so now,
They clapped their hands, as one would think, enough
    to make them sore,
While many swung their handkerchiefs, and others
    stamped the floor ;
And it seemed quite a while to me before the noise
    was done,
And singin' we had come to hear was cleverly begun.

I don't know what the matter was, for we were close
    at hand,
But there was not a single word that we could under-
    stand ;
We wasn't deaf, we're sure of that, but somehow every
    note,
No matter whether high or low, just wobbled in her
    throat
About like organs with a valve they call a tremolo,
And made me almost nervous, 'cause the music
    flickered so ;
But every time she finished up they clapped her an
    encore,
And brought her back so many times to sing and
    wobble more.

They say she spent four years away, I think 'twas at
  Berlin,
A-trainin' of her voice, I s'pose, to put the wobble in,
For Nature never makes a voice, of woman or of bird,
That trembles so (except from fright) as ever I have
  heard.
And even all the elements that whisper, roar or moan,
Have all of them got something like a grandeur in
  their tone,
That sends a thrill of pleasure to my senses and my
  heart,
But I can't say I relish this, if this is truly art.

She was a splendid lady, though ; her presence on the
  stage
Was all that ever need be asked, by any patronage,
And she could sing ! for once or twice she let the
  pucker slip,
And such sweet notes are seldom heard from any hu-
  man lip ;
And I kept wishin', after that, she'd let it slip again,
So she could sing the evenin' through in that de-
  lightful strain,
For there was music in her voice, as anyone could see,
Who had a half an ear for it, if she would leave it free.

But wishin' wasn't any good, the pucker was so
  strong,
From such persistent trainin' that it ran through all
  the song,

And we must grin and bear it, though it grated on
      our ear,
Since it was just the music which we come so far to
      hear ;
And yet my thoughts were busy with a sort of won-
      derment,
If that was just the mission on which music had been
      sent,
And if it had to flutter so, just like a wounded bird,
To charm a cultured audience, whenever it was heard.

And then I asked the question, if the Lord, who made
      the voice,
Had only latitude enough to take the single choice
Of that or nothin', when he made it, and though not
      the best,
It was as good as He can do, with means which He
      possessed.
Or did He leave it incomplete, with some divine intent,
That what He failed to give it, we ourselves should
      supplement,
And spend our time and money growin' valves with-
      in the throat,
To make the music better, by a quiver in the note ?

The only voice in Nature that a person ever meets,
Which has a jerky motion, is the sheep or goat that
      bleats ;
And no one calls that music, but the way which they
      express

Some sort of feelin' in them that is givin' them dis-
tress.
I s'pose I'll be unpopular for thinkin' as I do,
But I can't help it if I am ; I couldn't be untrue,
If all the world was standin' round, and coaxin' with
their eye,
Or clappin' hands, or stampin' feet, applaudin' of a lie.

LADIES' ENTRANCE.

We find a lot of places, in a certain line of trade,
Which show a vein of enterprise in signs they have
displayed.
The "fogy" style of business men who run a public
store,
Let all their customers go in and out a common door,
And seem to never have a thought that some would
like to buy
A certain class of dainty things a little on the sly,
And doubtless lose a lot of trade because they don't
provide
That timid customers be served a little to one side.

It seems to us commendable, that caterers for trade
Should make their place of business, where these pur-
chases are made,
As free from those embarassments which modest people
feel,
As possible, for buyin' what they wanted to conceal.

And it is not surprisin' that the ladies come to think
That what is awful good for men is good for them to
      drink,
And if the men who take their grog will drink behind
      a screen,
Who blames a modest woman if she'd rather not be seen?

But Nature don't discriminate, in anything like that,
Along the line of sexes, in her "lettin' out the cat,"
But has a means of tellin', in a certain way that shows,
The habits of the person in the face and on the nose.
And so it doesn't count for much, this tryin' to be sly,
For Nature isn't very long in tellin' what they buy,
And though they may discard alike the bar-room and
      the jug,
They haven't really learned the art of hidin' up their
      "mug."

But 'tisn't worse for women, if they happen to be dry,
To gratify their appetite, in what they choose to buy,
And get a little "frisky" from their purchase, now
      and then,
If they don't chance to gauge it right, than it would
      be for men.
And men don't think it's anything to stagger on the
      street,
And won't admit that they are drunk if they can keep
      their feet ;
And where's the sense of makin' such distinctions in
      the sex,
Because a woman drinks it, and receives the same ef-
      fects ?

We stand for sex equality, and with our humble pen
Demand for women all the rights accredited to men ;
They guzzle beer and whiskey with the keenest appe-
      tite,
And hover round the bar-room with an evident de-
      light,
As flies hang round a carrion, or anything that stinks,
To hear the smutty stories, and be ready for the
      drinks ;
And if there's pleasure in it, then it's meanness to deny
The same delights to women, or compel them to be
      sly.

If bar-rooms are a proper place for boys and men to
      throng,
It's proper for them all to take their girls and wives
      along,
And he's a scamp and puppy who will spend his
      money there,
For pleasure which he won't allow his girl or wife to
      share ;
A hog, without the bristles, or a sneakin', selfish cur,
Who loves his belly better, by a thousand fold, than
      her,
And who can blame the women, if they follow them
      for spite ?
But they are spoilin' half their joy, by drinkin' out of
      sight.

14

I'd be as independent, if I wore a petticoat,
As those who wear the breeches, and who know
    enough to vote ;
And if I wanted whiskey, I would go as straight as
    men
To places where they sell it, and would drink it there
    and then.
And if my beau or husband should object to see me
    there,
I'd raise my glass and drink his health, and say I
    didn't care.
I couldn't have the patience with their playin' fast
    and loose,
I'd teach them that the gander's sauce was sauce for
    Mrs. Goose.

You'd want to kill the brute who sat around his
    family board,
And crammed himself with everything he liked, or
    could afford,
While those whom he has sworn to love were left to
    go without,
And get as lean as Pharaoh's kine, while he was
    growin' stout.
But which is worse, to play the hog around his table
    there,
Or buy and drink what he denies his loved ones, any-
    where ?
Oh, woman, persecuted still, and cheated of your
    right,
We cannot blame you much to drink, we'd blame you
    less to fight.

CO-OPERATIVE.

Four hundred and sixty hard dollars brought in,
    At the simple request of our chief-of-police,
As the citizen's share of the prostitute's sin,
    And placed to the credit of virtue and peace,
To pay for the work of our shovel brigade,
    Or canceling other legitimate bills,
Which, but for this money would have to be paid
    From citizens' pockets, and citizens' tills.

How much of this money each person may claim,
    As his or her legal, proportionate share,
Depends on the values assessed to their name,
    Which fixes the burden each person must bear ;
But some of each dollar each prostitute pays
    Makes everyone's taxes, we're free to confess
(Reducing the volume of money to raise,
    By what they contribute) just so much the less.

The most of us claim to have something akin
    To manhood and virtue, and like to be thought
Above such a " brood " whose detestable sin
    These four hundred dollars and over have brought.
But the dividend from it, which comes every year,
    In spite of our innocent looks, will declare,
What few of us wish, we presume, to appear,
    Just what is our each individual share.

And so, by analogy, if we had more
    Of these sort of "citizens" here to "assess,"
(Amounts to be raised to remain as before),
    For every such person our tax would be less.
We leave it for some mathematical brain
    To give us the figures, provided they can,
How much this "contributing" portion must gain,
    Before we shall reach self-support, from the plan.

And how nice it would be ! oh, how nice it would be,
    To pay all expenses from profits we share
With "business" like that, while all other went free
    From burdens which they are expected to bear.
It may not be long, at the rate we've progressed,
    Before we shall reach such exemption from tax,
Because our municipal burdens shall rest
    Where men's hands have placed them, on feminine
        backs.

Of course, these "assessments" preserve our good
        name
    From any suspicion of whether or not
There rests upon each of us part of their shame,
    And whether our morals are tainted with rot.
The frequent and liberal fines which they pay
    Would take honest labor a long time to earn ;
And if we had laws that could send them away,
    To serve out a sentence, they might not return.

The newspapers, giving the name and the street
    Of each demi-monde, make them easy to find,
And so, while they're giving their readers a treat,
    Gives news and a free advertisement combined.
The system, for such it has gotten to be,
    Has in it what looks like a "devil's device,"
But the people will stand it as long as they see
    That the "privilege" pays them a liberal price.

DOGS IN THE MANGER.

Who hasn't heard the story of the crabbed cur that lay,
To suit his own convenience, in a manger on the hay ;
And when the weary, patient ox, returnin' from the
        field,
Essayed to enter for his meal, his place refused to
        yield ?
The hay was nothin' more to him than just a cozy
        nest,
On which his worthless carcass might recline awhile
        to rest,
But to the toil-worn ox it meant his wasted strength
        renewed,
Had not the thoughtless, selfish cur deprived him of
        his food.

A thousand other curs than he have manifested spite,
To keep earth's weary toilers from their Heaven-pur-
        chased right,

And been as much a "squatter" where they had no
     right to be,
And held their place by virtue of their inhumanity.
Some do it out of meanness, with the sense to com-
     prehend
The sufferin' which they entail, but try not to defend ;
While others are so stolid, we are driven to infer,
They do it more from instinct than of forethought, like
     the cur.

We don't attempt to figure to which class those men
     belong,
Who give their ballots, year by year, to legalize a
     wrong.
They must be either stolid, or be vicious through and
     through,
To vote against humanity, as many of them do ;
If they can't reason how effects must follow after cause,
They may be irresponsible for havin' vicious laws,
But if they have sagacity to see what they portend,
No other word than "cussedness" their actions can
     defend.

And yet these things in breeches can repeat, as if by
     note,
That "women will unsex themselves if they attempt
     to vote ;
They can't maintain their purity if they shall ever
     mix
With fathers, sons and husbands, in the nations poli-
     tics."

But they can meekly suffer, and not have a word to
    say
About the cruel burdens they must carry day by day,
'Til joy is turned to madness, and 'til hope has found
    it's bier,
But not—by all that's holy—must she ever interfere.

But bless them, they are not un-sexed by givin' birth
    to boys,
To fill up the depleted ranks where alcohol destroys ;
" If they are loyal mothers," so the politicians prate,
" They'll do a better service to the nation and the
    State,
And make themselves more potent for the triumph of
    the right,
By keepin' up their prayin' than by joinin' in the
    fight."
" The hand that rocks the cradle," is the proverb that
    they quote,
" Is mightier for conquest than the one that holds a
    vote."

There might be such conditions, but are yet too far
    away
To justify the pretty things which they are pleased to
    say ;
But women's sad experience for years and years gone
    by
Has branded this assertion as a savage, cruel lie.
These "doggies in the manger," while they nest up-
    on the hay,
Refuse to eat of it themselves, but keep the ox away ;

The curse of drink, these men who vote *might* outlaw
    if they *would*,
While those whom they keep disfranchised would do it
    if they *could.*

We talk about the Ganges, where the heathen
    mothers throw
The babes from off their bosoms to the crocodiles be-
    low ;
And send out missionaries of the humble Christ to say
To every heathen mother that there is a better way ;
While christian motherhood at home must sit and
    weep beside
Her husband or her sons debauched, and both her
    hands are tied ;
The fathers do the throwin' of their little ones away,
In christianized America, while mothers weep and
    pray.

You call the fathers heartless for the awful work they
    do,
And point to rows of victims, but it wouldn't quite be
    true.
They, like the heathen mothers, in their heart of
    hearts deplore
The sacrifice demanded by the God whom they adore ;
But, like her in devotion, they will not withhold
    their best,
If politics demands it, in the babes from off the breast ;
And so, to save the party, let their sons and daughters
    sink,
With somethin' like a fortitude, beneath the waves of
    drink.

The cur was not responsible for bein' born a cur,
Nor for defendin' "squatter rights" in things he
      might prefer ;
The heathen mother's blindness is a thing to rather
      claim
From christians and philanthropists their pity than
      their blame ;
And so, perhaps, the fathers are within the party's
      grip,
That they are not responsible for bein' "on the hip."
We wouldn't judge them harshly, but we hope there'll
      come a day
When manhood will outgrow it's shell, and they shall
      get away.

And if they dare not do the things for which the
      women pray,
Perhaps they'll give their wives a chance by gettin'
      out their way ;
And if they do, ah, if they do, it won't be very long,
Before they'll hear the music of the grandest, sweetest
      song
Which ever floated upward from the human heart and
      tongue,
Since time began its cycles, and this hoary earth was
      young ;
The song of man and womanhood delivered from the
      reign
Of legalized damnation, for the traffic has been slain.

THE "CELLAR DOOR" VARIETY.

(The city police recently raided a sporting house,
which the daily papers mentioned as the "Grimes
Cellar Door," and the inmates were sent away to jail,
while several other houses of the same sort, run in
somewhat better quarters and style, were simply fined
and allowed to continue "business.")

It seems to make a difference what sort of craft they
     ride,
Among the class of people who possess a little pride.
A place may clearly be a "ranch" and glory in the
     name,
And have the courts and city press a heraldin' their
     fame,
And still not be considered as a thing to give offense,
Which is at all revoltin' to our higher moral sense,
If they are near the centre, and are run in decent style,
And promptly pay the "levies" on them every little
     while.

It doesn't seem to count for much that it's a slidin'
     scale,
From innocence and virtue to the "cellar door" and
     jail ;
And people even tell us that it's best to let them be,
Because a certain number are a real necessity.

And if they state it truly, then we haven't much to
        say,
Because, of course, it's better for the boys to let them
        stay ;
But don't let us be mean with those who happen to be
        poor,
And can't afford a better craft than just a " Cellar
        Door."

It wouldn't be surprisin' if they felt themselves op-
        pressed,
When, by judicial action, they're a scape-goat for the
        rest ;
For they know how their sisters, who can sail a better
        barge,
Have often pleaded guilty to the prostitution charge ;
And yet, because of reasons which it isn't wise to say,
Were left to carry on their " trade " while they were
        sent away ;
And they, no doubt, will wonder if the crime was any
        more,
Because their place of business was an humble " Cel-
        lar Door."

And we confess we wonder if it's true, as sometimes
        said,
That virtue in a man must mean his bein' old or dead ?
And then, again, we wonder what a high and regal
        place,
A fellow's manhood will assume before a lady's face,
If it is true, as some assert, that dens of infamy

In any city under Heaven are a necessity?
We wonder, too, if fellows who resort to such a place,
Would like to have their wives and sisters share in
    their disgrace?

We wonder if the persons whom the citizens elect
To guard the city's morals do about as they expect,
And when these "ranches" are assessed instead of
    bein' tried,
And punished, if found guilty, whether they are sat-
    isfied?
We think, however, that their hands are on the public
    pulse,
And when it's throbbin' strong enough, will show it
    in results.
But then we face the question, "Who is ready to
    make war,
And smirch their name and fingers with a system they
    abhor?"

And if the disposition of the "Grimes' Cellar Door"
Shall prove a faithful prophecy of justice yet in store
For others of the same bad ilk, a justice long delayed,
We think we're justified to hope we're on the upward
    grade.
And yet we hardly dare rejoice to any sort of tune,
Lest our congratulations prove a little bit too soon;
But wait to see if prostitutes with carpets on their
    floor,
Shall join the same procession with the homely "Cel-
    lar Door."

IF I WERE YOU.

If I were you, with what I know
   Of Jesus' power to cleanse from sin,
I would not keep him waiting so,
   But quickly rise and let Him in,
         And make Him room.

If I were you, I would not dare
   To treat the Lord of Glory so,
While living only by His care,
   As though He were a common foe,
         And nothing more.

As though the offers of His grace
   Made so repeatedly to you,
Might be flung backward in His face,
   From year to year, your whole life through,
         And not harm you.

If I were you, I think I'd say,
   And be so thankful that I could,
" Yes, Lord ; come in my heart to stay,
   And make me what Thou seest good,
         And right away. "

If I were you, and had not known
  The peace His blessed presence brings,
I'd make His offered help my own,
  And rest beneath His sheltering wings,
      And there remain.

I'd test His willingness to save
  A man in middle life like me,
And not continue Satan's slave,
  If Jesus Christ would make me free,
      If I were you.

If I were you, I would not spurn
  The only ransom for my soul,
Nor would I long delay to turn
  To Him whose touch could make me whole,
      And keep me clean.

I would not wish to see how far
  The way of death I might pursue,
Because of what His mercies are,
  In sparing me what was my due,
      If I were you.

But with the years which hurry by,
  So many gone, so few to come,
I'd think it worth my while to try
  And make secure a heavenly home,
      If I were you.

For, cling to this life as we may,
    And having eyes, refuse to see,
The wheels of time will not delay
    To whirl us on to destiny.
                Both you and me.

If I were you, I would not wait
    Till all my life's best years were past,
For though not, possibly, too late,
    'Twould make the noblest work the last
                And incomplete.

And since the Lord had died for me,
    Simply because He loved me so,
To make His great salvation free,
    I'd take the gift He would bestow,
                And be so glad.

OLD JACK ON A SPREE.

The creak in the snow, and the sting in the air,
    And the shivers that roam, like a spirit set free,
Would indicate "Jacky" has thrown off his care,
    And gone by himself on a real "jamboree."
And not, as his wont, for a night and a day,
    With a bee in his hat, and some frost in his hair ;
But this time he seems to have broken away
    For something that looks like a regular "tear."

And my, what a rampage it turns out to be,
    Continuing on while the weeks run together,
With blizzards and storms that are frightful to see,
    While the changes are more of the same kind of
        weather ;
The mercury (bless it) is not all to blame
    For falsehoods it's telling to every beholder ;
For if it had room to go down, 'twould proclaim,
    Almost anywhere, it was some degrees colder.

His heart, if he has one, appears to be stone,
    Untouched by the want and the woe he is flinging ;
Or his ears must be deaf to the piteous moan
    Of the helpless whom he is so cruelly stinging.
But what made him wild ? and how long will it last ?
    Are things which his subjects are anxious to know ;
And will he be ever the Jack of the past,
    And tread his old ways after spreeing it so ?

The secret, we think, of Jack's losing his head,
    Was coming so soon into such an estate,
Where empire would seem to be unlimited,
    And power to rule correspondingly great ;
And passion for conquest so kindled his zeal,
    To hold in his thraldom whatever he met,
His pleasure, and not what his subjects might feel,
    Has seemed to possess him, and make him forget.

So much like a mortal, as doubtless he is,
   A little brief power is soon tyranny ;
He thinks not and cares not how many may freeze,
   If he but himself may enjoy liberty.
But truants or tyrants alike find their way
   Hedged somewhere before them with stronger de-
      fences,
And so we are hoping that some sunny day,
   Old Sol will bring Jack to his sober senses.

And when he reflects, will his memories sting,
   For pains which he shot from his merciless quiver,
Which pierced like an arrow, and severed the string
   Of many a life-cord forever and ever ?
Or will he believe, that for all the distress
   His fingers have scattered, the rest he has given
The bosom of Nature will more widely bless
   The millions who suffered, and thus make it even ?

IN MEMORIAM, MRS. DR. BULLOCK.

From such a life of ceaseless, patient pain,
Too thoughtful and too gentle to complain,
   To such relief of sudden, perfect rest,
Is such transition that to those alone,
Who pass, like her, through both, can it be known,
   And needs immortal powers to be expressed.

And when the gracious Father takes His child,
It is not heartless to be reconciled,
    And say, in spirit, "Lord, Thy will be done;"
Her years of suffering may well suffice
To win consent of strongest human ties,
    That weary feet, like her's, should cease to run.

And yet the Father sees it not amiss
That tears should come at such a time as this,
    To minister the magic of their balm;
While even through their mists they may behold,
Through gates ajar, within the Shepherd's fold,
    Enough to turn our sorrow to a psalm.

No more the throbbing pulse of pain shall beat,
Through years of intermittent cold and heat,
    No more her patient spirit needs to long
For loosened pinions that are plumed for flight
Beyond the boundaries of human sight,
    Nor sigh to join in love's immortal song.

The largest liberty is her's at last,
With earth's contingencies and perils past,
    And all of immortality ahead;
Then wherefore should we make our plaintive moan,
Though, for a time, we tread the way alone,
    And wherefore think or speak of her as dead?

Ah, no ! not dead, but more alive than we,
Who still are cumbered with mortality,
   And to be envied rather than deplored ;
From earthly limitations disenthralled,
By what we mis-call death, she hath been called
   To be forever and forever with the Lord.

THREE MINUTES LATE.

We hurried through our breakfast, and we skipped
     our morning prayer,
Because the old clock told us that we had no time to
     spare ;
Our guests must reach the station, for the early
     morning train,
Or else be disappointed, and our haste would be in
     vain.
We gathered up their parcels while they kissed a fond
     adieu
To those whom they were bound to by a friendship
     old and true,
And started for the depot at a most ungraceful gait,
To find, when we had reached it, we were just three
     minutes late.

We felt chagrined a little, and our guests a good deal
    more,
But it had never happened in our history before ;
The cause of it was plain enough, the clock, which
    all along
Had measured off the time so well, this once had done
    it wrong,
And we had been misguided, just a little by it's tick,
Without the least suspicion that 'twas playing us a
    trick ;
It's silent hands had pointed wrong upon the dial-
    plate,
And it's unspoken falsehood made us just three
    minutes late.

How often does it happen that some unsuspecting feet
Walk up to disappointments which they're unpre-
    pared to meet,
And fail to reach the objects which their hopes have
    had in view
Because the guides they've followed haven't been ex-
    actly true ?
And how it often happens that they have to bear the
    pain
And weariness of waiting, if they do not wait in vain,
At some of life's way-stations, and have many hours
    to wait,
For other opportunities by getting there too late.

It makes a bit of difference, as many persons know,
Alas, by their misfortunes, in what paths their feet
      shall go ;
And then it makes a difference with destinies of men,
Not only *where* they start to go, but quite a difference
      when.
The saddest disappointments, and must give the
      keenest pain,
Will be to reach life's junction for the last out-going
      train,
And find, instead, a notice that they must forever
      wait,
Because they reached the station just a little while
      too late.

THE WAY OUT.

Brother, what if forces press you,
   Which are out of your control,
Till they grievously distress you,
   As they surge against your soul ?
Has the purpose which has planned it
   Hedged you in with pain and doubt,
Only to forever stand it,
   Leaving for you no way out ?

Must the strivings be extended,
   And the conflict waged in vain,
Till the earth-life shall be ended,
   With no victory to gain ?

Must the ceaseless round of sighing
　　Not be broken by a shout,
And deliverance, by dying,
　　Be, for you, the one way out?

Tell me, which way are you turning
　　Inward thought and outward gaze;
With or without clear discerning
　　Of the world's divergent ways?
Sweeping only with your vision,
　　Things suggesting only doubt,
Noting not, with what precision
　　Upward ways will lead you out?

Looking downward, vision reaches
　　Little farther than your feet,
While the narrowness it teaches
　　Turns things bitter, meant for sweet.
Looking up, at once discloses
　　Visions which dissolve your doubt,
And a way which interposes
　　Nothing to your soul's way out.

Ah, this world is wider, brother,
　　Than the lines which compass you,
And in helping one another
　　Is distilled life's honey-dew.
Looking upward is ascending,
　　With a bounding step and shout;
All earth's bright and dark things blending,
　　To provide a sure way out.

What if skies above you lower?
　　What if pulses throb with pain?
What if all Satanic power
　　Vex you o'er and o'er again?
Is not Heaven still above you,
　　Throwing faith-lines all about,
With the God-man there to love you,
　　And assure a safe way out?

Souls were never made to cower
　　In the conflicts which arise,
But, with cumulative power,
　　Made for winning victories.
Have you often been defeated?
　　Then, my brother, face about;
Lest your failures be repeated,
　　God and Heaven are your way out.

SHALL WOMEN VOTE?

Things are not as they used to be
　　Away back in the distance,
Before a thousand things we see
　　Had ever an existence;
For woman seemed a cipher then,
　　And man the only figure,
And even when allied with men,
　　They simply made men bigger.

But Time seems giving her a " boom "
　　Of quite another spirit,
For every place is making room,
　　According to her merit.
Abreast with men, in every race,
　　Though often a beginner,
She runs with dignity and grace,
　　And scores the mark, a winner.

She demonstrates that she has brains
　　For every requisition
Of home or State, to hold the reins
　　In high or low position.
But we, the men who make the laws
　　(Simply because we love her),
Enact them with a little clause,
　　Which holds ourselves above her.

It takes such mighty grasp of mind
　　To see one's obligation,
Where interests are so combined,
　　As in a State or nation ;
That only those of stronger mould
　　Can hope to measure to them ;
Or seeing them can be so bold
　　As fearlessly to do them.

So here we wisely draw the line
　　(And frequently by quoting
Some scripture, giving right divine
　　For man to do the voting).

.

Man may be " verdant " as can be,
　　And thus our logic teaches
That his superiority
　　Is less in brain than breeches.

CHORUS.

She has the art to win the heart
　　Of clowns, as well as sages,
Knows how to rule a king or fool,
　　Has done it through the ages ;
And yet, alas, it comes to pass,
　　No matter what her merit,
That clowns and fools of all the schools,
　　Her rights can disinherit.

THAT REVENUE.

(It appears from the reports of the Commissioner of
Internal Revenue of the United States, for the fiscal
year ending June 30th, 1887, that the receipts from
fermented liquors were $21,022,187, an increase over
the previous year of $2,245,446.   United States In-
ternal Revenue tax was paid upon 23,121,526 barrels
of fermented liquors, an increase for the year of 2,410,-
583 barrels.—(International Royal Templar, Sept.,
1887.)

Twenty-one millions of dollars a year,
On twenty-three millions of barrels of beer !

And here he has stopped, but why doesn't he tell
Of lives it has wrecked, and of souls sent to hell,
Of wives it has widowed, and hearts that have bled,
Of prospects now blighted, and hopes that are dead,
Of virtue polluted, of murder unhung,
Of schemes to decoy and to ruin the young?
Ah! why don't he tell of the blight and the shame
Which clings to the innocent bearing the name
Of some of these victims of some of this beer,
That's swelling the treasury year after year?
He tells of this "industry," speaks of its gain,
But says not a word of the sorrow and pain
Which come as a fruitage, as certain as fate,
And spares not the lowly, the gifted or great.
And how they applaud it, this wise statesmanship,
Which wrings out the millions from ruin's soulless
     grip;
And tell us that taxing will regulate sin,
And drive out the wrong while the money flows in.
Yet here is the record, "two millions a year
Of increase in numbers of barrels of beer."
But nothing is hinted, no single word said,
How many more victims of drinking are dead,
How many more widows and orphans are made
For this two million dollars of revenue paid?
Oh, shame on the manhood which sells for a price
Indulgence for wrong and a license for vice,
Which pockets the money and closes its eyes
On all this dark picture, and hears not the cries
Of wailing humanity rising to God

That He will deliver in peace, or with rod !
But how many dollars will pay for the woe
Which out of these millions of beer barrels flow ?
How long will it take, at this rate of increase,
'Til taxing and license shall cause it to cease ?
How many more victims of drink must be slain ?
How many more hearts must be throbbing with pain ?
How many more orphans and paupers be made,
Before we shall see what a price we have paid ·
For revenue gathered in year after year,
From millions on millions of barrels of beer ?

"YE ARE THE BRANCHES."

A branch, indeed, and He the vine !
What hinders, then, the life divine
 Thrilling and throbbing through my heart,
'Til every fiber feels the beat,
And tingles with the strength and heat
 Which such a current can impart ?

Am I a branch, and He the vine ?
Why, then, in weakness need I pine,
 As though my strength had no supply ?
Why fruitless hang from year to year,
The shoots and tendrils which appear,
 Bearing but leaves to fade and die ?

A branch of that Eternal vine !
How can my trusting heart repine,
   However smitten by the blast ?
For though awhile bowed down with pain,
His strength shall lift me up again,
   Brighter than though they had not passed.

A branch, and He the living vine !
What mighty privilege is mine
   To catch the throbbings of His heart,
And feel the precious currents flow,
As through each little twig they go,
   Giving His life to every party.

A living branch, and Christ the vine !
How perfectly the two combine ;
   Yet all the fruitage which appears,
He does not even ask to share,
But lets his feeble branches bear,
   To glorify their fleeting years.

Oh, feeble branch, with such a vine,
Was ever privilege like thine ?
   Well may your bounding pulses thrill,
That by the grafter's magic art
You feel the throbbings of His heart,
   And see the purpose of His will.

Henceforth let only gladness shine
From every branch of this great vine,
 In pendant clusters from each stem;
And when, at length, the golden year
Of God's great harvest shall appear,
 Each cluster shall become a gem.

SHOVEL OUT.

The blizzard had its lessons, which were borne upon
  the wind,
And dropped at many a door-step in the thought it
  left behind.
It reigned a very monarch, with an undisputed sway,
And chained the wheels of commerce for a nation in a
  day ;
It made its crystal messengers a conquering brigade,
To force its proclamation for a general blockade,
And brought to every homestead with a morning song
  and shout,
The truth that they were captives, if they didn't
  shovel out.

It's just an illustration of another sort of " blow,"
Which hedges many lives about with something else
  than snow,
And turns a pleasant prospect, which is everything
  that's fair,
Into a sudden tempest with obstructions everywhere ;

And makes of their to-morrow, what might seem like
    prison walls,
Heaped high with disappointments where the mass of
    driftage falls ;
But rarely, like the blizzard, is there heard the warn-
    ing shout,
That those within are captives, if they do not shovel
    out.

And yet the fact is patent, there's a power in the spell
Of sudden great reverses that may prove a captive's
    cell ;
A sort of soul concussion seems to paralyze the brain,
And bind the will with fetters, and to kill out hope
    with pain,
And look out on the driftage in an aimless sort of way,
Heaped high about the door-sill from the hopes of yes-
    terday ;
While ears are dull and listless to the voice of any
    shout,
That there may be deliverance if they will shovel out.

But, brother, if a blizzard has swept over all your
    plains,
And piled the driftage higher than your upper window-
    panes,
A tiling lifted from the roof will bring the welcome
    sight,
That everywhere, outside of you, the world is full of
    light,

And you can, with your shovel, and a purpose brave
    and stout,
With sturdy and persistent work, soon tunnel your
    way out ;
But if you wait the action of time's equalizing law,
You'll have a lonely waiting, and may die before a
    thaw.

OLD JACK, THE ARTIST.

There are divers inspirations, each of which have
    given birth
To marvelous achievements by the toilers of the earth.
Some, born to please the fancy, have their mission in
    display,
And some are harnessed stoutly to the work of every
    day.
But there's a subtle something in the breezes of the
    North
That proves an inspiration for old Jack to sally forth,
And with his brush and pencil, paint the fancies of
    his brain
In most exquisite tapestries on every window-pane.

Just how he guides his pencil in the shadows of the
    night,
To form the perfect outlines, and the perfect shade
    and light,

And how he does the grouping of the flowers, ferns
    and trees,
And makes them blend so perfectly, with such ap-
    parent ease,
And all in such profusion, is away beyond the ken
Of all the etching masters of the scribbling sons of
    men ;
And yet this careless fellow gives his brush the freest
    reins,
And scatters beauty everywhere without apparent
    pains.

Sometimes he coyly takes his brush in broad daylight
    and tries
His skill upon the window-panes before our staring
    eyes,
And does it so adroitly that we rack our clumsy heads
In wonder where or how he gets the fleecy paint he
    spreads,
And how he carries models, as he must, within his
    brains,
For all the wondrous etchings on the countless win-
    dow-panes,
And why he never sketches either mountains, plains
    or seas,
Or forms of living creatures with his flowers, plants
    and trees.

And he's an out-door artist ; when the weather suits
    his mood
He leaves his window-sketching and betakes him to
    the wood,
And in the same profusion every bough and twiglet
    drapes
With curious festooning in the most delightful shapes,
He mingles pearls and diamonds with his white
    wreaths everywhere,
And has the skill to make them from the elements of
    air ;
And he's as swift as skillful, for it takes him but a
    night
To drape the woodlands everywhere in robes of spark-
    ling white.

And not a single picture hangs in all his gallery,
To bring a blush to innocence for any eyes to see ;
He copies nature truly, yet with nothing woven in
To be a sly suggestion that he ever thought of sin.
We see in all his pictures such a mirror of his heart,
As one in love with nature and a master of his art,
And stand in awe before them, as we hear the silent
    speech
Of what is pure and beautiful that whispers out from
    each.

A KNOTTY QUESTION.

Five drunks, the daily papers say,
In the Recorder's court to-day,
    And each adjusted by a fine ;
Ten dollars each were paid by three,
Two paid the regulation fee,
    And all to help your tax and mine.

But who'll be kind enough to tell
How law, which makes it right to sell,
    Can also make it wrong to buy ?
Or if to buy is not a sin,
Can anyone explain wherein
    It's wrong to drink, if one is dry ?

If right to sell and right to buy,
These rights must certainly imply
    The right to drink what they had bought ;
And where law makes the crime appear
Is not to this deponent clear,
    Unless it lies in being caught.

Another point confronts us here :
Some legal mind can make appear,
    Perhaps, to those of obtuse brain,
How taking, legally, the bread
From hungry mouths which must be fed
    By public tax, can be a gain.

And some of us would like to know
What fruit must come of what we sow,
    In this reform at which we play,
If those of tender years shall see
This farce of inconsistency
    Enacted over year by year.

What wholesome lessons will they draw,
Teaching the sanctity of law,
    Where sense and conscience both rebel ;
And what foundation for a state
Will such convictions educate
    In hearts such statutes must repel ?

IS IT FAIR ?

(The reason why the guests were not arrested, who
were found at the houses of prostitution, when they
were raided by the police recently, was because there
is no law for their arrest.—Morning Times.)

Was ever his Satanic Majesty known,
By cunning devices and cheats all his own,
To lure the unwary in pathways of sin,
And when they're in trouble, to stand back and grin ?

Are virtue and chastity led to their fall
Without man's intrigue, or designing at all,
That victims of lust, which men's passions create,
When ruin is wrought, should be left to their fate ?

While those at whose instance their feet went astray,
Be they morally rotten and vile as they may,
Can hold up their heads and continue "scott free,"
While she bears the burden of their infamy?

How like the "Deceiver" for those who are strong
To lure on the weaker in ways that are wrong,
And when retribution would make them atone,   ·
Slinks out, for the weaker to bear it alone.

What shame for the sex that makes laws for the two,
Yet leaves, for their own, such a loop to crawl through ;
The first to transgress, yet when crime has been done,
Law says, of the two, that their's only may run.

Oh, chivalry ! born for defense of the weak,
Hast thou grown degenerate, so thou canst seek,
With spirit so craven that devils might blush
To own thee as kindred, the weaker to crush ?

If laws are not righteous, still let them be fair,
And make the transgressors their own burdens bear,
And not make the strong a contemptible sneak,
By throwing the guilt of his crimes on the weak.

HOW IT PAYS.

The hands on the dial of Time yesterday
Were pointing again at the fair face of May,
   To welcome her back to her place in the year ;
While she, the coy maiden, to cover her face,
Unfastened her delicate curtains of lace,
   That we might not witness her smile or her tear.

For what should she see on the first day she came,
But scenes which should mantle her fair cheeks with
       shame,
   And send the hot tears of regret to her eyes ;
For, glancing in many a court-room, she saw
How manhood is ruined according to law,
   And then how the law measures out penalties.

Our city, it seemed, had its record maintained
In the number of " drunks " which it's court had ar-
       raigned
   To answer its charges, and ask how they plead ;
When three answered " guilty " with nothing to pay,
And " justice " decided to send them away
   To languish in jail for the county to feed.

Five months is the aggregate term of the three,
Which justice and law gives these culprits board free,
   With nothing to do but to eat and to sleep ;

Beside the expense, to the county, in fare,
And fees to the officers taking them there,
   And running the house which the sheriff must keep.

Then, added to this, are the officers here,
Police and Recorder six hundred a year,
   To watch for these culprits, and send them away ;
Extorting, perchance, if by some sort of squeeze,
A part of the culprits can muster the fees,
   The statutes prescribe such offenders shall pay.

The dollar or so which the poor wretches spent
To get up the drunk over which they were sent,
   Lies calmly at rest in the dram seller's till,
While we, who pay taxes, must pocket our shame,
And bravely accept our defeat in this game,
   And *play we are happy to settle the bill.*

IT IS BETTER.

Better to dwell in a mansion fair,
   Under the light of the blazing throne,
Than wandering homeless here and there
   With nothing but life to call her own.

Better to join the ransomed throng,
   Safe in the Shepherd's upper fold,
Than carry the burdens borne so long,
   Till flesh was feeble and bent and old.

Better to enter the pearly gate
  Swinging ajar for such as she,
Than longer to struggle, and suffer, and wait,
  Hoping and sighing for liberty.

Better to travel the golden street
  Of the King's highway, with her youth renewed,
Than carry the load, on her weary feet,
  Of a heartless child's ingratitude.

Better to know, as she knows at last,
  What are the joys and rest in store,
Now that the trials of earth are past,
  Waiting her spirit forevermore.

Better the bliss of an answered prayer,
  Better the light of eternal day,
Than bearing the burdens of earthly care,
  And wearing the fetters of mortal clay.

Better to sing in the Heavenly choir,
  Better to know as she is known,
Better the gift of her soul's desire,
  Waiting before the eternal throne.

PERHAPS.

(Respectfully commended to the attention of all
railroad and street car officials.)

Perhaps 'twas all a blunder for the Lord of Hosts to
  say
That men of every nation should observe the Sabbath
  day.
Perhaps He was mistaken in regard to human need,
Not knowing all about it, when this statute was de-
  creed,
Or culture may have so refined the present race of men,
That they don't need the discipline which people
  needed then ;
And yet the same old statute stands, and in the same
  old way,
Requires of every person that they keep the Sabbath
  day.

Perhaps it may be well for men to trample under feet
A statute whose enactments they consider obsolete,
And in their work or pleasure do exactly as they
  please,
Instead of being hampered by a lot of old decrees ;
And yet no intimation has been given, anyhow,
That those old obligations are not just as binding now,
As when, amid the thunders of the mountain, every
  word
Was graven on the tablets by the fingers of the Lord.

Perhaps the railroad companies may make God's holy
       day
Contribute to their income in a strictly business way,
By planning their excursions, and by running extra
       trains,
Without a single pretext but the increase of their
       gains,
And flaunt out their defiance to His solemn code of
       laws,
By using what He sanctified, for such a selfish cause ;
And still expect His blessing on their business day by
       day,
Because, perhaps, some members of their corporations
       pray.

Perhaps it may be well for them to hire a band to play,
To help degrade the Sabbath to a common holiday,
And lure the people somewhere for a sort of aimless
       stroll,
Instead of, as He meant it, for the helping of the soul,
And prostitute an ordinance He meant for human
       need,
To minister to pleasure, and the lust of human greed :
And like enough these companies may finally outwit
And break down all the statutes of the Lord, before
       they quit.

Perhaps the obligation of the people to obey
The code received on Sinai have long since passed
       away,

And men are independent of Jehovah's discipline,
As well as independent of the penalties of sin,
And ask no odds of mercy, but are altogether free
To follow inclination, whatsoever that may be ;
And reading their advertisements would lead one to
      infer
That railroad corporations have concluded that they
      were.

SUPPOSE.

An occasion that will doubtless be memorable in
this city will be the appearance of the most able
American orator now living, Col. Robert G. Ingersoll, who lectures at the Shattuck Opera House, Saturday evening, May 5, on "What Must We do to Be
Saved?" Col. Ingersoll's increasing years and his
devotion to his home life and his law business make it
unlikely that he will ever again visit this city after
this lecture.

The Colonel in this lecture disputes the inspiration
of Matthew, Mark, Luke and John, as in his lecture
entitled "Some Mistakes of Moses" he disputed that
of the author or authors of the Pentateuch. He also
proposes a system of practical benevolence which he
holds to be more beneficial to man than any presented
in the four gospels. His lecture, while antagonistic
to the belief in faith and revelation, sets forth the supreme nature and beauty of goodness and kindness.
The Colonel advocates free thought, "with malice toward none and charity for all."

Suppose the Colonel could make plain
That christian faith is all in vain,
   And souls are never saved by grace ;
What other formula or creed,
Which meets the world's acknowledged need,
   Has he to offer in their place ?

The gospel scheme has stood the test,
Filling the souls of men with rest,
   And its adherent lived and died,
Through all the ages of the past,
Triumphant, even to the last,
   Having a faith which satisfied.

Suppose the Colonel could destroy
The christian faith and hope and joy
   From human lives by what he said ;
Would there be less of fear and pain
Because their faith in God was slain,
   Without some better thing instead ?

The Colonel is no friend to man
Till he can formulate a plan
   Better than that which he attacks,
Giving a brighter, surer hope ;
Lifting the human spirit up
   With certainty the other lacks.

Matthew and Mark will still be read
After the Colonel shall be dead,
   And Luke and John maintain their place,
Pointing the hopes of men above,
And telling of the matchless love
   Which brought salvation to our race.

SING! SING! SING!

Sing of the boundlessness of grace
Which gladly took the sinner's place,
And died to save a guilty race.
          Sing!   Sing!   Sing!

Sing of the love which stooped so low,
To rescue from eternal woe,
His enemies that spurned Him so.
          Sing!   Sing!   Sing!

Sing of the Christ, who loved so well
The souls of men, deserving hell;
He lifted them from whence they fell.
          Sing!   Sing!   Sing!

Sing of the King who ever lives,
Sing of the grace He freely gives
To every soul who truly strives.
          Sing!   Sing!   Sing!

Sing as you climb the Heavenly way,
Sing all your cankering cares away,
Sing of His love from day to day.

Sing ! Sing ! Sing !

Sing of the triumphs which you meet,
Sing as you see your foes retreat,
Sing, with the world beneath your feet.

Sing ! Sing ! Sing !

Sing, though the whole round world go wrong,
Sing, though your foes be swift and strong,
Sing, with the Christ-love for your song,

Sing ! Sing ! Sing !

Sing 'til the earth shall fade from sight,
Sing with the chorus robed in white,
Forever sing your soul's delight.

Sing ! Sing ! Sing !

CENTENNIAL ANNIVERSARY OF THE SET-
TLEMENT OF THE CANISTEO VALLEY,
SEPT. 23, 1890.

(This poem was written by request of the program
committee, but owing to the length of program was
omitted.)

We press our inquisitive eyes to the screen,
To see, if we may, what there is to be seen
A century backward, where lips are so still ;
They give us no answer, inquire as we will ;
And records of what there was here on the scene,
With the tramp of a century rolling between,
Are so incomplete, though we haply have some
That much of it still is the speech of the dumb.
Yet we see in our thought how this valley appeared
Before there was yet a square foot of it cleared,
Or ever the white man its surface had trod,
But just as it came from the fingers of God.
A forest unbroken, except by the stream,
Which winds, like the thread in some doll-baby's seam,
With scarce a design or conception of grace,
But crooked and zig-zag as fancy could trace ;
And into the shadows of this solitude,
The glimpses of sunshine could rarely intrude ;
And when they succeeded would send in a beam,
Which glimmered and rippled like waves in a stream,
While under the shadows of hazel and pine,
Were mosses, and moosewood, and berry, and vine,

And sometimes a literal tangle of fern,
And shadows where "fox-fire" would constantly burn;
And where, at their pleasure, the pheasant and grouse
Would drum on their log, or contentedly browse ;
Where the cry of the panther or bound of the deer
Were nightly resounding in dame Nature's ear ;
And the howling of wolves, and the grunt of the bear
Were common as nightfall, and heard everywhere ;
And the snakes with their hissing, or rattling tail,
Had only each other to fear or assail ;
And the marshes which spread out their water and bog
Were vocal at mid-day with croaking of frog.
No great stretch of fancy is needed to-day,
To see in the distance which stretches away,
The crouching of wild beasts on branches that leaned
Just over this place where we now are convened,
And stealthily watching the steps of his prey,
Which, heedless of danger, is wending this way,
Till he suddenly leaps from his perch, and has lit
On the back of a deer, just where some of you sit,
And the blood of his victim has reddened the dirt,
Which just now is covered by some lady's skirt.
The "deer-lick" which hunters remember, was near,
And drew other wild beasts, as well as the deer,
And the moccasined feet of the savage could tread
As noiseless as panthers that crouched overhead ;
And one of them crept from his cover near by,
And silently vowed that this panther should die,
And scarce had the blood of his victim been shed,

When the hunter's bow twanged, and the creature lay
    dead,
And a wild whoop of triumph went rolling away,
That his arrow had bagged both the beast and his prey.
We know not the place where the wigwam has stood,
Or the trail of their feet, as they wound through the
    wood ;
The sight of their villages shows not a trace,
Which white men can recognize, marking the place,
Where their corn dance and war dance have often oc-
    curred,
And the savage's bugle, the war whoop, was heard.
But we know that the red men had villages here,
At least during favorite seasons of year,
That they fished in these waters, and traversed these
    hills,
And slept in these valleys, and drank from these rills ;
But we know not the place where their dead have been
    laid,
Nor the tribute which savage affection has paid.
A century backward, the white man appeared,
And straightway the forests began to be cleared ;
The axe of the woodman swung on day by day,
And little by little it wasted away ;
The openings widened on valley and hill,
As the kings of the forest bowed down to their will ;
And so with the tramp of the years, it retires
Licked up by the tongue of a century's fires.
The wild beast and savage long since disappeared,
And homes have been built on the broad acres cleared ;

And cities and hamlets are spreading today
In place of the wilderness now passed away ;
And little, it seems, is there now left behind
To vividly call up the past to the mind,
And educate new generations to see,
What fathers bequeathed to their posterity.
Their courage and patience and hardy good sense,
Which toiled for the future with small recompense ;
Their sturdy endurance, which still persevered,
Through forests like these till their homesteads were
        cleared ;
With breeches of buckskin, and shoes of the same,
They toiled, like the heroes they were, without shame;
While the wives in the cabin, with distaff and flax,
Had spun for the shirts which they wore on their
        backs.
They were proud, but 'twas not of clothes which they
        wore,
But proud of the fruit which their industry bore,
And well would it be if we still emulate
This virtue of those whom we commemorate.
We look where we will and see monuments left,
Hewn out by the blows which these woodmen have
        cleft,
More lasting than marble or granite upreared,
In the beautiful fields which their industry cleared.
We come not to honor these heros today,
But rather a tribute of homage to pay ;
Their rugged achievements are chaplets more grand
Than e'er can be woven by their children's hand ;
We shall honor them most if we follow the trend

Of their simple lives, and their virtues extend.
The change of a century, what would the men,
Who wended their way into these forests then,
Say now, could they glance with one sweep of their
    eyes
On the wonderful fruitage of their enterprise?
One link there seems left of this century-chain,
Not pleasant to think of, their serpents remain.
Yet even these snakes are a different brood
Than swam in these waters, or crawled through the
    wood,
Whose dens were the rocks, or some sheltering roots,
For these have their haunts in the dram drinker's boots.
Some work yet remains for the loyal and true,
Which our fathers have left, knowing not what to do ;
And the thinkers and workers of this present age
Need the courage and wisdom of saint and of sage,
That the legacy left us, the pride of to-day,
Be not, by our foolishness, bartered away.
Perhaps some are musing of what they might see,
Could they witness the close of the next century ;
But we venture a guess that a century on,
The progress will not be by muscle and brawn,
Like much of the past, but will largely be brought
By the culture of heart and the triumph of thought ;
And the steps of our progress henceforward shall move
In the higher and nobler arena of love,
And that much that we see now, and see to deplore,
Shall then be a trouble and menace no more ;
And of this we are sure, they will certainly be
A century nearer earth's great jubilee.

UNCLE ALVIN CRACKIN' NUTS.

I seldom see the early frosts but memory will recall
The jolly times we used to have when nuts began to
 fall,
And how we boys would sally forth, with each a cup
 and sack,
And sometimes get as many as we cleverly could
 " back."
And when the nuts were nicely cured, and when the
 winter came,
We interspersed the crackin' them with many a jolly
 game,
And jokes as well as nuts were cracked, and hearty
 laughter rang,
And sometimes frolics mingled with the merry songs
 we sang.

But crackin' jokes and crackin' nuts I found a different play,
For, sometimes, in the latter sport my thumb got in
 the way,
Or else the hammer dodged the nut and fell upon my
 thumb,
And almost pounded off my nail, or made a blister
 come ;
And then, almost invariably, I hit the nut a whack,
Which made it spin across the room, or else it made
 it crack,

And that relieved my temper, and, of course, relieved
        the pain,
And after swingin' it a while, went crackin' nuts again.

But that was years and years ago, and though I'm
        gettin' gray,
And life takes on a meanin' which is somethin' more
        than play,
I relish yet the crackin' nuts, though of a different
        kind,
And not with stone and hammer, but with efforts of
        the mind.
And some, I find, crack easily, and one can get the
        " pit,"
If there is any in it, and enjoy the eatin' it,
Without a lot of hammerin', because the shell is thin,
And offers small resistance to the kernel held within.

But now and then I find a nut, and sometimes quite a
        batch,
So fortified within their shell they prove more than a
        match
For any poundin' I can do or skill I know about,
To get the rind and shell removed, and get the kernel
        out.
I know there's lots of wiser men in each community
(If not, I'm sorry for the place) than I pretend to be,
And so I'd like to ask if they can any of them crack
The hard shelled nut which I have got reposin' in my
        sack ?

The one that puzzles me the most, and I esteem the
    worst,
I think I'd better give to them to try their skill on
    first,
And if they prove a match for that, I'll hand the bal-
    ance out,
For they may each contain a truth the world should
    know about.
The nut is this : how soon can we put any wrong away,
By sellin' it the privilege of stayin' on, for pay ?
If crime can pay the premium that's charged it by the
    State,
Does money that's obtained from it, its evils miti-
    gate ?

Will money in our coffers pay for all the manhood
    slain
By alcoholic murderers, which license lets remain ?
Or will it heal the broken hearts, or dry the flowin'
    tears,
Or make the wail of misery like music to our ears ?
Or will it, by the part it takes in government, set free
The voters of the nation from responsibility ?
Does God, who loves the souls of men, esteem them
    any less,
Because the parties weigh them out to win a brief
    success ?

And here's another nut for them : if christian men can
      pray
That God will rid our land from rum, then vote to
      have it stay ;
Or if they do not pray at all, but vote to legalize
This traffic, which is certainly " the sum of villainies,"
How high will such a prayer ascend, and what does
      such a vote,
When stripped of all its party ties, and party names,
      denote ?
Is God or party uppermost in such a heart and mind,
Which helps his party to success, but leaves his Lord
      behind ?

PERTINENT QUESTIONS.

(To be answered at the polls)

How long will it take to accomplish a work,
If those we set at it the labor shall shirk ?
Or if they keep toiling, but day after day
Keep working exactly the opposite way ?
What good will it do to keep looking aghast,
As citizen voters with ballots to cast,
At wrecks we are meeting on every highway,
While casting our votes that the whiskey shall stay ?

Will the faces we make, and the sighs that we have,
Do much for the sorrowing hearts that must grieve ;
Or make it less easy for unwary feet
To fall in the traps which are lining the street ?

Suppose we, as christians, shall fall on our knees
And pray the great Father, as much as we please,
To take this temptation and peril away,
And then cast our vote that the traffic shall stay ?

Does God answer prayer, as the most of us pray,
In a go-as-you-please sort of good-natured way,
And do what we ask Him, while we ourselves stand,
Refusing to help Him, by lifting a hand ?
If whiskey and beer are so good, in their way,
How silly, to Him, must it seem, while we pray ;
But if they are evil, as most of us think,
Why need we ask Him what to do with the drink ?

What "gush" to bewail, as the most of us will,
The fate of the fellows they so often kill ;
Why not place a rooster just up at the head
Of the notice which tells that another is dead ?
It stands, as a symbol, to let people know
Of triumphs achieved, and not simply to crow ;
And when one has fallen, why not have displayed
An emblem which tells of the progress we've made ?

For this is an "industry," so says the law,
And men the "material" when in the "raw,"
But after they pass through this government mill,
Whatever is left is fit only to fill
A shroud and a coffin and dishonored grave.
But where is the sense in our trying to save
The boy or the man from his ignoble fate,
Since death to the man is a gain to the State ?

And since we have government whisky to drink,
What sort of a scheme would it be, do you think,
If we could have, also, a government cow
To furnish us milk, and a government sow
To furnish us pork, and a government hen
To lay us a government egg now and then?
And why may not farmers be suffered to keep,
And share in the profits of government sheep?

Ought whiskey and beer to be burdened with tax,
And carry the government lashed to their backs,
When such minor things as our sugar and tea
Can come to our tables essentially free,
While the government even a premium pays
On all the production of sugar we raise?
But who pays the tax in the end, do you think,
The fellows who sell or the fellows who drink?

And now, after all, can it ever be wise,
On any conditions, to make merchandise
Of the vices of men, for the beggarly sums
Which we must divide with the bars and the slums?
What kind of humanity is it which preys
On the weakness of men for the profit it pays?
What sort of economy is it which thrives
On the wasting of wages and ruin of lives?

How long would it take us to sewer the town,
And pave it besides, and to pay it all down,
If we had the money that goes to the tills
Of the landlords now running our government mills?

And when shall we reach a more prosperous state,
Unless we shall do it by changing our gait?
We can if we wish, we can sweep it away,
And it need not take longer than next voting day.

Or will it be better to let the thing run
In the shiftless-go-easy way which we have done,
By frequently throwing these fellows a sop,
And own that we're under, and they are on top?
Well, we are the people, nobody's to blame,
If we shall decide to continue the same ;
And, may be, by waiting, these men will conclude
To throw up their business and learn to be good.

But how nice it would be if the mothers could know
That the sons which they bear would be suffered to grow
To a manhood more noble than just to be killed,
To furnish a market for whisky distilled.
But the needs of the " business " at present demands
As costly oblations as this at their hands,
And leaves them but little redress, but to wait,
And hope, amid trembling, or weep at their fate.

Men, also, have feelings and gravely deplore
The needs of the " trade " and the perils in store
For the young men and boys, and if they understood
How to save *both the boys* and *the business* they would ;
But the wisest of statesmen can't find out a way
To rescue the boys and to *make whisky pay*.
And it don't take a statesman a long time to choose
When it comes down to *dollars* or *boys, which to lose.*

WHISPERS FROM THE FARM.

(Prepared by request of officers of the Farmer's In-
stitute, and read before them at their annual meeting
at Hornellsville, N. Y.)

I've been a farmer since so small and weak
I could not reason, understand or speak ;
My first industrial tendencies displayed—
Based on the statements which my mother made,
And which, in candor, I may not gainsay,
With all the evidence the other way—
Was drawing milk, and if results can tell
Of past success, succeeded fairly well;
For you, as farmers, know that, otherwise,
I scarcely could have reached my present size.
No law is more apparent anywhere
Than stinted growth from early scanty fare.
I may not be, in any proper sense,
A dairy product, having recompense ;
But, through the ills by which it is beset,
The dairy keeps its hold upon me yet.
No dainty beverage, by man distilled,
A place so prominent has ever filled,
In this great world of multiplying need,
To slake its thirst, its hungry millions feed ;
No fairy ever pressed her dainty lips
To sweeter nectar than the urchin sips
From his tin cup at morning or at night,
Nor with the half his healthful appetite.

No epicure can quite complete his dream
Of things he longs for, without thoughts of cream ;
Itself alone, or skillfully combined,
By culinary wisdom of the kind
These wives and daughters gracefully display
Around the kitchen table, day by day,
In articles, to mention which would need
A longer list than we would care to read,
Or you to hear, but all of which unite
Their grateful relish to the appetite.
And then the juicy grass and fragrant hay
These thrifty farmers' wives have stored away
In jars and pails and tubs of various size,
To wait the market or their own supplies ;
Transformed, 'tis true, by nature's alchemy,
And their own handicraft and industry,
In bulk and color from the forms they bore,
And with a flavor they had not before ;
But grass and hay essentially the same,
However called by more euphonious name,
If one could see them, would afford a sight
To fill a healthy eater with delight.
What matter if the butter which you spread
In golden flakes upon your snow-white bread,
Has twice been chewed before ? Or when you drink
Your glass of milk, whoever stops to think
Where, and by what a process it was brewed
Into such pleasant, healthful human food ?
And who among you would be less at ease,
While masticating some one's creamy cheese,

Because, in open field or glimmering shade,
Not long before, it was a simple blade
Of common grass, and some one's patient cow
Was eating it, as you are doing now?
And yet 'tis grass, you and your cow are fed
On the same substance and are comforted.
She ate at first, and lodged within her hide
Were potent forces gravely occupied
Distilling, shall we call it? grass and dew
Into a healthful beverage for you.
How was it done?   Well may we question how;
Our only answer is, the cow, the cow.
You press the grass, and straightway will be seen,
Not milky whiteness, but a livid green;
You taste its juices, scarcely will you find
The faintest flavor of that grateful kind
You taste in milk.   And so we constantly
Are taking in an unsolved mystery.
We call it nature: is the mystery less
Because of our reluctance to confess
What we know not, and play with words to hide
Our ignorance, and so seem satisfied?
And what is nature but the complex wheels
Through which our God himself to man reveals?
And you, as those whose labor brings you near
To nature's heart, should have the quickest ear
To catch the many pulses, as they trill
Through every form of life, and thus fulfill,
By agencies like these, His gracious plan
Of being felt and recognized by man.

What other calling, in which men engage,
At present or in any previous age,
Links them so close, in all their round of toil,
With His great power, as those who till the soil?
This hungry world would famish but for you,
And death would thrust his fingers through and
        through
The busy wheels of every enterprise
Which thrill and throb in countless industries.
God's hand is opened, and you stand to take
What He bestows for His creation's sake,
And pass it on, through mart, and press, and mill,
To the remotest purpose of His will.
Nature's high priests, what lesser rank have they,
Whose chosen calling is but to convey
Her lavish bounties with the utmost speed
Into the gaping mouths of those who need?
An humble calling, is it, thus to stand,
Taking these royal gifts first from her hand ;
Feeling the pulse of nature's throbbing heart,
As she unbosoms, that she may impart
The rarest of her gifts, for you to spread
Wide as the need of those who must be fed?
Call it the noblest, and be satisfied
To be in such a mission occupied.
Inquire of her, and she will not conceal
The things it may be wisdom to reveal ;
But gladly makes a confident of those,
Who equal confidence in her repose.
Knowing her secrets, you shall more and more

Unlock the treasures of her store ;
Scorn her, and, maiden like, she will recoil,
And be avenged in unrequited toil.
What other labor is less commonplace
Than your's, which brings you daily face to face
With constant miracle?   Can you explain
How dirt and sunshine, heat and air and rain
Can so combine that they become the meat
Of every living thing which needs to eat?
Take man alone, and see a table spread
Three times a day, for those who must be fed ;
Three double rows, close seated side by side,
Three times around the world, and satisfied :
Then think how this great throng shall re-appear,
Not once alone, but daily, year by year,
And find, no matter how they multiply,
Enough each day to amply satisfy.
Then count the herds which must supply them meat,
And measure, if you can, the rice and corn and wheat,
Which, through a year, must furnish them with
        bread,
And weigh the tons of butter which they spread ;
And then the milk which this great throng will pour
Would shame Niagara, with its rush and roar ;
Pile up the fruit, what pyramids you rear
To feed the hungry world a single year.
Where figures fail, let fancy lend her wings,
To scale the mountains of such other things
As lavish nature on her sons bestows,
Of every vegetable thing that grows.

Whose hands but yours become the open door,
Through which these mighty resources must pour?
Call it ignoble, will you, thus to stand,
Taking these gifts, so fresh from nature's hand,
And be her ministers, the world to feed,
With everything provided for its need?
Suppose you tire, with none to take your place,
What other industry can feed the race?
Nay, if combined, how could they all supply
That sustenance, without which man must die?
And if so needful, surely it must be
Clothed with no meagre share of dignity.
True, ignoramuses may under-rate,
And over-reaching avarice create
Monopolies, which may awhile oppress;
But time and patience will these wrongs redress.
And yet, these money-barons and their tools,
With their half-brothers, ridiculing fools,
Are prompt as other men to pass their plate
To share the bounties which you help create.
Humble, it may be, but pray tell us what
Of valued service to the world is not.
Surely, foundation things are frequently
Destined to rest in some obscurity;
The loftiest monuments which ever rise
Can only stand upon what underlies;
The cap-stone revels in the light of day,
While the foundation may be hid away.
The cap-stone, still, might totter from it's seat,
And fall in fragments at the gazer's feet,

And yet, the monument might still endure
For generations perfectly secure ;
But let disaster happen to the walls
Which forms its base, and the whole structure falls.
It may be pleasanter to occupy
A place which will attract the public eye,
But it is better for the world that we
Be occupied in useful industry ;
And you can ransack all creation through
To find another thing which man may do,
Which is itself sub-stratum for them all,
And without which they everyone must fall.
Not all, perhaps, but few, who eat their fill
From fruitful fields your hands have helped to till,
Have thought enough to half appreciate
Their obligations for the things they ate.
But your reward lies not in human praise,
But in the golden harvests which you raise,
And in your contribution to the need
Of even the ungrateful whom you feed ;
Even as He, who lets His blessings fall
Unstinted and ungrudgingly on all.
No more important work, for human weal,
Is wrought on any great industrial wheel,
Than that which furnishes the daily bread
Of which our whole humanity is fed.
And here we pause.   Has this gigantic plan
No other, deeper interest to man,
Than to the oxen which we feed and drive,
That we should be content to simply live ?

Have we no other and no greater need
Than that which meat and milk and grain will feed?
Has nature taxed her utmost energies
To crowd her storehouse full of all supplies
To feed the nations who are here to-day,
And who, to-morrow, will have passed away?
Does God's great plan, in wheeling worlds in space,
Of which our earth is one, no thought embrace
Beyond the careful giving of supply
Of creature wants until the creature die?
Rather, is not the mighty system wrought
Around the central, all-pervading thought
Of immortality ; and things of sense
Become important, but as incidents
Which may or may not helpfully control
The tendencies of an immortal soul?
As stairways, up which human feet may climb,
From the material to the sublime,
This round of daily, sometimes irksome toil
Should be transformed by those who till the soil.
Who, if not you, within whose constant sight,
The silent, potent elements unite,
In God's great laboratory, to prepare
Food for the nations, out of earth and air,
Should stand in awe, amid such majesty,
And hear and do His pleasure cheerfully?
And when, at length, you reach life's eventide,
With burdens dropped, and duties lain aside,
Who, if not you, will have the keenest zest,
After your toil, for His eternal rest?

18

BUILD UPWARD.

Build upward, my boy.   Opportunities grand
Will come within reach of the place where you stand ;
But they, like the fragments of time, are so fleet,
They're gone, if not seized and placed under your feet ;
And you, as a builder, will need to be quick,
To grasp and to use them, as masons do brick ;
Not hodful at once, but a brick at a time,
So life's opportunities help you to climb.

Some builders, my boy, have begun at the top—
A clink, and some dust, and you hear something drop ;
And scattered about, in the place where they fall,
Are fragments of what was a beautiful wall.
So character-builders too often find out
That only the fragments lie scattered about,
The character gone : they began at the top,
And built only ruins by letting things drop.

Build upward, my boy, by adopting the plan
The great Master-builder has drafted for man.
The wrecks which lie scattered about should suffice
To teach you a lesson and open your eyes.
They planned for themselves, and they built as they
          planned,
A structure as shapeless and worthless as sand.
God can not be mocked, and the ones who build down
Will build but a dolt or a villain or clown.

CHORUS.

Build upward, build upward, build upward, my boy,
And choose a foundation Time can not destroy ;
And if, in your work, you let anything drop,
Let it be what would hinder your reaching the top.

GOOD FOR THE BLUES.

The most of men have, now and then, a tussle with
    the "blues,"
Which, while they stay, can paint a day with most
    despondent hues ;
And they can vex the fairer sex, in spite of wit or
    grace,
And send a rain of tears to stain the sweetness of
    their face.
But Nature knew just what to do in every such attack,
To turn the night to broad daylight, and bring the
    sunshine back ;
'Tis music's charm that can disarm this robber of our
    peace,
And make the "blue" of every hue, while it remains,
    to cease.

But some will say they can not play, and some they
    can not sing,
And how can they drive "blues" away with weapons
    they can't swing ?

But, bless you, man, you surely can, for nature don't
    impart
A gift so grand with partial hand, needed by every
    heart.
Songs do not spring from *lips* that sing, but come
    from out the *soul*,
And lips and voice have not a choice but let the music
    roll.
Your *soul* may lift her royal gift, in accents high or
    low,
Though lips are mum and voice is dumb, and bid the
    shadows go.

WE'RE ALL IN IT.

We're doing things we disallow,
    And saying things by us unspoken,
While often ready to avow
    No wrong is done, no statute broken.
We've all attested our delight,
    Through those by whom we're represented,
In being at a rooster fight,
    And to the broken law consented.

The most of us would spurn the thought,
    If it was even intimated
That our own virtue could be bought,
    Or possibly was over-rated ;

Yet everyone of us receive,
   Through an unwilling contribution,
Our paltry taxes to relieve,
   The shameless hire of prostitution.

We shudder at the awful deeds
   Of men whose hands are red with slaughter,
And sigh for every heart that bleeds
   Over a murdered son or daughter ;
And yet do we not sanction still
   That policy in legislation
Which gives our full consent to kill
   The very flower of the nation ?

The mighty burden rests somewhere
   For all this vast amount of evil ;
And we can hardly roll our share
   Over upon the poor old devil.
Nothing but cowardice can shrink
   From facing this great obligation
To purge the vice of lust and drink
   Out of the city, State and nation.

"PLENTY OF BEER ON THE GROUND."

The artist was early this morning, with chalk,
With which he has given a voice to the walk
(And not one, but many) by making it say,
"A game of base ball at the fair ground to-day,"
And every few rods you are certain to meet
The same thing repeated right under your feet ;
And under it sometimes this sentence is found,
That "there will be plenty of beer on the ground."

It seems, the world over, a recognized law,
That a cause or a scheme must have something to
        "draw ; "
And the work of the artist proclaims that he knew
The force of this truth, and has kept it in view
When he skillfully placards around on the walk
Its greatest attraction in letters of chalk ;
For he makes the stone say, in no uncertain sound,
That "there will be plenty of beer on the ground."

The day may be hot, and the players may sweat,
And need, to refresh them, to have something "wet ; "
And even the crowd, who work hard (with the eye),
In watching the players, may get warm and dry ;
And it's thoughtful of him, in advance to proclaim
To players and all who shall witness the game
(And, of course, those who read it will pass it around)
That "there will be plenty of beer on the ground."

But, somehow, we wonder if he didn't lie,
Or had not, while chalking, a "stick" in his eye ;
For, reading it over, it has a queer sound,
As he tells us that "there will be *beer on the ground.*"
" Be beer on the ground !" what a nice thing to say,
While players play on, and the stuff runs away !
What nonsense ; don't go there expecting to find
Much " beer on the ground," save, perhaps, in your
      mind.

A CHURCH MOTTO.

One soul a week for Jesus,
   Our watchword ought to be ;
And then with passionate desire,
Our every heart should be on fire,
    This glad accomplishment to see ;
And night and day our earnest cries
Upon the wings of prayer should rise,
    That God will set the captives free.

Thus consecrated, we should be
More watchful and more quick to see
    And recognize our fellow's need ;
And winter's cold or summer's heat
Would not retard our willing feet
    From scattering the precious seed.

One soul a week should be our aim,
And in the blessed Master's name,
　　Without consulting with our fears;
Our lips should not be slow to move
With messages of hope and love,
　　To pour in unconverted ears.

Suppose we shall be satisfied
With this experiment untried,
　　And we shall be content to feel
That our own hearts and lives are pure,
And our salvation is secure,
　　Without a further care or zeal?

Suppose, that with the harvest white,
We do not labor as we might,
　　And some of it be left to rot ;
And afterward it shall appear
That here and there a wasted ear,
　　If we had sought, we might have got?

Suppose that we consult our ease,
And labor only as we please,
　　Amid the world of human need ;
Will it be just as well at last,
When opportunities are past,
　　That they received so little heed ?

One soul a week for Jesus,
  Suppose we all shall say ;
And then, not only in our prayer,
But in our labors here and there,
  Should watch for chances day by day,
With men and women whom we meet,
Within the homes, or in the street,
  To tell them of this better way ?

Would it be long before our zeal
Would make these men and women feel
  That we were anxious for their sake ;
And would the seed we thus should sow,
Going among them to and fro,
  Within their hearts no rooting take ?

Suppose we aim at nothing more
Than swinging like a common door ?
  We might accomplish what we aim ;
But would our lives be strong to bless,
And make the sins of men the less,
  Because we bore a christian name ?

The sons of men do not attain
Successes on a higher plain
  Than they deliberately plan ;
And then are driven to confess
To bitter failures, more or less,
  When they have done the best they can.

Then what successes shall we see,
If we shall drift on aimlessly?
   But if unitedly we seek
For fruitage all along our way,
Who is there that shall dare to say,
   We may not win one soul a week?

This motto, then, let us inscribe
Upon the banner of our tribe;
   And then as much as in us lies,
Make it our constant care to seek
And gather in one soul a week,
   For "whoso winneth souls is wise."

SKATING ON THE CANACADEA.

Never before, since the old creek run,
Has it furnished the youngsters with so much fun,
As since "Old Jack" for the ten days past
His icy mantle has over it cast,
And held its gurgling waters below,
While the boys have cared for the falling snow,
And with careful pains kept it scraped away,
To clear the field for the evening's play.

And play it has been, for when shadows fall,
They gather like troopers at bugle call,
Their shoulders slung with an armor of steel,
If not for the breast, for the toe and heel;

And the glassy stream has a heart of glee,
As he tips his cap to them merrily,
And chuckles behind his icy grate,
To witness the joy of an evening's skate.

And the boys and girls, as they swiftly skim
Over the ice-field spread by him,
Have scarcely a thought to whom they owe
The joy which is thrilling their young hearts so ;
And scarcely a fear that the words they say
His lips may babble abroad some day,
And make them blush for the "spooney" word
That the sly old elf has overheard.

And yet, no doubt, if we knew the truth,
He is so in touch with the heart of youth
That nothing could tempt him to betray
A single word that their young lips say ;
For he knows, we think, that much of the charm
Of an evening's skate lies in some one's arm ;
And a part, at least, of it's pleasure is traced
To the gallant support that surrounds a waist.

But aside from that, there's a healthful joy
In a lively skate for a girl or boy ;
While the young blood courses from limb to limb,
As they poise on the polished steel, and skim,
Like an arrow shot from a sinewy bow,
Across the ice-field, to and fro ;
And we watch from the bridge that is over them hung,
With a wish, half acknowledged, that we were young.

"WHAT WAS JOHN WESLEY'S IDEA IN ORGANIZING THE CLASS SYSTEM?"

(A paper prepared and read at a class leaders' convention held at Corning, N. Y. The subject was given the writer by the program committee.)

This question may read plain enough, but when it is
    defined,
The answer will be difficult and delicate, combined.
It asks of us to traverse through a century or more
Of history behind us ; then it asks us to explore,
Not simply what the founder of our methodism
    wrought,
Which made his name immortal, but interpret what
    he thought,
And read the inner workings of his great, heroic soul,
Which moves among the nations still, reaching from
    pole to pole,
And marshalling for conquest with a most consummate
    skill,
The loyal sons and daughters of the Lord Almighty,
    still.
We pause before a question which might tax an
    angel's pen
To give a truthful answer to the minds of common
    men ;
Yet one thing is apparent, and we have the right to
    say,

He thought to help his fellow men to climb the
    heavenly way.
He knew by hard experience at many a time and
    place,
"That this vile world," as he had sung, "was not a
    friend to grace,"
And that the constant warfare which the saints of God
    must wage
Would need such re-inforcement as "would conquer
    Satan's rage,"
And kindle in their bosoms such enthusiastic fire
As burns amid the conflict where the hosts of hell
    conspire ;
And makes them shout in triumph while baptized in
    flood or flame,
And sing their hallelujahs in their great Commander's
    name.
He knew, for he had tasted, of the help it would af-
    ford,
To talk with one another of the dealings of the Lord ;
How timid hearts got courage, and the feeble were
    made strong,
As well by faithful witnessing as by the voice of song :
And how a soul had often, from what might have
    been a rout,
Been helped to scale the parapets, and hang their
    banners out.
And yet he scarcely could have dreamed without a
    prophet's ken,
The half of what the system of the class would do for
    men ;

No thought of all its helpfulness along the century,
Back over which we travel, could the mind of Wesley
     see ;
He saw, indeed, the present ; how it worked from day
     to day,
Girding the soul for obstacles it met along the way ;
He saw it as a factor which could keep alive the zeal
Of christian men and women to defy the foeman's
     steel,
And stand with elbows touching upon every battle
     field,
Or fight or fall for victory, but never, never yield ;
But hardly could he have believed, if it had been fore-
     told,
The matchless possibilities the system would unfold ;
How from its small beginnings, where its banners
     were unfurled,
'Twould spread within a century until it filled the
     world.
He might have had impressions that a system which
     could bless
The witnesses for Jesus, where they joyfully confess
Their purposes to serve Him, and to rest upon His
     word,
Should then, and ever after, have the blessing of the
     · Lord ;
But where the blessing of the Lord would ultimately
     lead,
We doubt if any thought of it entered his busy head.
The system had its origin, not first in Wesley's
     thought,

But in the deep experience which in his soul was
    wrought,
By his complete abandonment of self, and will and
    all,
To hold himself in readiness to heed the Spirit's call,
And go wherever bidden, without questioning the
    plan,
And use his utmost efforts to lift up his fellow man.
Thus wholly given up to God, his constant attitude
Toward the Spirit's movings made them quickly
    understood,
And while his soul was quickened to perceive the
    Spirit's will,
His thought was quickened, also, in the methods to
    fulfill.
And so the church we honor owes a vastly higher
    mead
To Wesley's deep devotion than it owes to Wesley's
    head.
Clear as his mental powers were, much of their clear-
    ness came
From having in his nature such an all-consuming
    flame
To spread abroad the knowledge to the needy sons of
    men,
That Christ was their salvation, and that he could
    save them then.
The scriptures tell us plainly, while all holy men
    unite
To give it their endorsement, that their "entrance
    giveth light."

Without their inspiration in the heart of Wesley then,
He might have lived his four score years, and died
    unknown to men.
He owes his immortality on the historic page,
Not to his brilliant intellect, as poet, scholar, sage,
But to his flaming zeal for God which filled him
    through and through,
And which enabled him to build more wisely than he
    knew.
How else can God make use of men, until they thus
    shall give
The best that may be in them, in the humble lives
    they live,
To do the work He gives them in the manner He
    shall show,
And let the Spirit lead them in the ways He'd have
    them go ?
Men may accomplish something, and may get a
    brilliant name,
And carve it on the tablets of the world's enduring
    fame,
By purely human efforts, in a worthy enterprise,
And sometimes be applauded by their fellows to the
    skies ;
But who among them ever, like our Wesley, have
    achieved,
Without an inspiration from the truths which they
    believed,
Such mighty benefactions for so many of his kind,
By any institutions they have planned, and left be-
    hind ?

The answer to the question asked, " What was the
    leading thought ? "
Is answered far more clearly by the mighty things he
    wrought,
Than they were ever answered by the feeble voice or
    pen,
Of even those who tower far above the most of men ;
An answer which the ages are repeating o'er and o'er,
And which uncounted millions shall repeat forever
    more ;
The thought of helping others by the means which he
    had found,
Had ministered a strength to him, and helped to
    hedge him round,
Amid his human weakness, while exposed to Satan's
    power,
And brought the sunshine through the rifts in many
    a trying hour,
And set his pulses thrilling with a courage which de-
    fied
All forces which opposed him, and a joy which satis-
    fied.
Well will it be for christians, of whatever faith or
    name,
If they can catch the spirit and a measure of that
    flame
Which makes the name of Wesley such a tower of
    strength to-day,
And covers it with glory which shall never pass
    away.

And such, the scriptures tell us, "waxeth valiant in
    the fight,"
Where "one can chase a thousand ; two, ten thous-
    and put to flight,"
Defy the powers of darkness, make the alien armies
    flee,
And hasten on the coming of the world's great jubi-
    lee.
Perhaps it may be questioned whether Wesley's active
    mind
Foresaw the church's future, where the system had
    declined,
Until, as at the present, its distinctive features stood
No longer as a blessed link of christian brotherhood ;
But in the face of history, as marvelous as true,
Of her magnificent advance, and what she has passed
    through
To reach her high position as the foremost church on
    earth,
She casts aside the spirit which presided at her birth,
And gives to christian testimony but a meager place,
To help her new-born children to maturity in grace.
But if he did foresee it, such a mind must have dis-
    cerned
Enough of peril in it to have made him feel con-
    cerned
About the church's future ; for declension here must be
A lapse from vital piety toward formality.
And such it has been proven, where the "class" has
    fallen down,

Much of the old-time zeal for God and power are un-
      known.
Churches increase in numbers, while their power to
      help and bless,
Measured by old-time standards, are as surely growing
      less ;
While God's unchanging promises are evermore the
      same,
The church's zeal for mighty things is manifestly
      tame.
So much organization, of a wheel within a wheel,
To barely keep in motion taxes ordinary zeal ;
A forward movement anywhere, on almost any line,
Takes super-human effort and a zeal that is divine.
Sometimes, thank God, we see it yet, but we should
      be surprised
At things that would be possible with her less organ-
      ized.
Simplicity was Wesley's thought, and to it he ad-
      hered,
And from it came the mighty works which every-
      where appeared;
God gave it His endorsement, and the powers of
      darkness quailed,
And single-handed conflicts with the hosts of hell pre-
      vailed.
Simplicity in worship : let the founder's spirit fall
Once more upon her membership, and consecrate us
      all ;
Let love divine inspire us with a kind of zeal which
      dares

To put some expectation in the spirit of our prayers,
And venture somewhat farther than our fleshy eyes
    can see,
And go wherever bidden and expect a victory.
If Wesley can look down from heaven upon our
    halting gait,
And see our little courage, while the golden chances
    wait,
For grasping mighty conquests in the cause for which
    he fought,
It might be interesting could we know just what he
    thought.
We may not turn interpreter, and undertake to-day
To be a mouth for Wesley, and to tell what he would
    say ;
We may not quite imagine how his earnest soul
    would feel,
After a century in heaven, and what immortal zeal
Would burn in every utterance his holy lips would
    frame,
If we could catch the message which he doubtless
    would proclaim ;
But sure as immortality, his words would neither aid
Or countenance in any way a thought of retrograde.
What he advised while in the flesh, that men should
    push their way
Through every obstacle they met, we think he still
    would say,
But say it with an emphasis unheard by us before,
And still point upward through the way " that shin-
    eth more and more."

And if this institution has been honored of the Lord
Beyond all computation, why should it not be re-
    stored?
Why may we not expect the power to dwell within
    the form,
If lives are just as earnest and our love is just as warm?
What Nehemiah shall arise and thrill us with his call
To help remove the rubbish, and re-build again the
    wall,
And set up ancient land-marks which are lying in de-
    cay,
More eloquent of ruin than of victory to-day?

THE PREACHER'S REMINISCENCE.

Beside my fire in cozy chat, one blustering winter day,
An hour or two the preacher sat, while memory
    strolled away,
And led his footsteps back again, over the way they
    came,
Until, unconsciously to him, his face was all aflame
With that same fervor which had thrilled those whom
    he'd stood before
In many a schoolhouse, where he'd preached, or sick
    bed he'd bent o'er,
Telling the Saviour's wond'rous love and mighty
    power to save,
And tinge with glory and with hope the darkness of
    the grave.

Ah, memory ! when she takes the reins, she goes at
    such a pace
That often e'er she calls a halt she gives us quite a
    chase ;
And so the preacher followed on, sometimes beside
    the bed
Of dying christians, who had found a pillow for their
    head
On that great bosom which has throbbed in pity for
    the race,
And from its depths has opened up a fountain of His
    grace :
Sometimes he tarried by the grave, where last good-
    byes are said,
And comforted, as best he could, the mourners for
    their dead.

Sometimes he led his willing thoughts back to the
    blessed place
Where, down the years which he had come, wond'rous
    displays of grace
Had often visited the work his hands had tried to do,
And set the Spirit's seal on scores of weeping souls
    anew.
"But greatest of the wonders wrought," he then
    went on to say,
"Was in Uriah's oldest girl, before she passed away.
You know he drank, and drank so hard—kind-hearted,
    though, and free—
And when the girl got very sick the old man came
    for me.

"Of course, I went, and read the word, and pointed
    out the way
As plainly as I could to her, and then I knelt to pray,
While old Uriah and his wife both knelt beside the
    bed,
And wept as if their hearts would break, while on my
    knees I plead
That God would show His mercy there and cleanse
    her soul from sin,
Take doubt and trembling from her heart and put His
    peace within ;
And some time, in a day or two, I don't exactly know
Just when it was, the answer came, the Lord per-
    formed his vow.

"I went to see her once or twice, and each time heard
    her say
She had the clearest evidence her sins were washed
    away ;
And one day, when my forenoon's work I thought
    was nearly done,
I saw the old man coming with his horses on the run.
He stopped before my shop and said, in his excited
    way,
'Come, brother Charles, I've come for you ; get in
    without delay.'
'It's noon,' I said, 'and dinner time ; but, then, of
    course, I'll go ;
Besides, I'm in my shirt-sleeves now, and can't go
    looking so.'

"'Dinner!' he answered; 'brother Charles, it will
     not do to wait;
Before you got your dinner it would surely be too late.
Borrow a coat, or go without.   The poor girl fails so
     fast
We almost tremble at each breath, lest it should be
     her last.'
In borrowed coat I got aboard, then how the horses
     flew,
And made the quickest two-mile drive, I think, I ever
     knew.
We found her failing fast, indeed, but calm as sum-
     mer day,
And, smiling, she gave me her hand, and then asked
     me to pray.

"And when the prayer was ended, and we'd risen
     from our knees,
We saw a sight before us that a mortal seldom sees:
Her pallid face was all aglow with a glory not its own,
But must have been reflected from the everlasting
     throne.
In accents which I can't forget, she uttered this re-
     quest,
With heaven's music, evidently, thrilling through her
     breast:
'I want you all to help me sing, "We'll Gather at
     the River;"'
And clear and sweet we heard her voice, without a
     break or quiver.

"And when the last words of the hymn had floated
    out in song,
She said to all the weeping ones, in tones distinct and
    strong,
'Now I must kiss you one by one, and bid you all
    good-bye,
And want you each to promise that you'll meet me in
    the sky.'
And so the farewell words were said, the dying lips
    were pressed,
Until each weeping friend in turn was tenderly ca-
    ressed.
'Father,' she said, when all had come, 'has not some
    one been missed?
I think there must be some one else whose lips I
    haven't kissed :
Ah ! brother Charles, you haven't come ; I want to
    kiss you, too ;
Your prayers and words have helped me so, I can not
    pass by you.'
And when I felt the parting kiss of that triumphant
    girl,
I felt my spirit lifted up toward the gates of pearl.

"Her work, we saw, was finished then, and with a
    peaceful smile
She calmly waited her release—only a little while ;
In thirty minutes from the time we knelt beside her
    bed,
Her triumph was completed, and we saw that she was
    dead.

And when I stood beside her form, upon her burial
    day,
It was not hard for me to think of something good to
    say ;
Nor was I much surprised to hear a man I'd known
    for years
Say, 'Charles, you beat yourself to-day,' and say it
    through his tears.

"And though I've stood so many times beside the bed
    of death,
And seen them smile, and heard them shout with
    their expiring breath,
I never seemed to look so far within the gates of pearl
As when they opened wide that day for old Uriah's
    girl :
No triumph ever seemed so sweet as when the angels
    came
And bore the drunkard's daughter home in chariot's
    of flame.
Ah, well !" he said, as he arose and started for the
    door,
"It don't hurt either you or I to talk these seasons
    o'er."

WHEN I AM DEAD.

Somewhere, along the coming years,
 That mystic gate I have not seen,
 Swinging so silently between
The known and unknown hemispheres,
 Shall let me pass in, to explore
 The realities of that fair shore ;
  And round my form it shall be said
  By those who gather at my bed,
   That " he is dead."

" What has he left ?" will be inquired
 By persons who do not relate
 In any sense, to my estate,
Almost as soon as I've expired ;
 And by that question simply mean
 The hoarded things which may be seen,
  With scarce a thought concerning bread
  With which the souls of men are fed—
  When I am dead.

What shall be left ? Ah, if I could,
 I would not choose to so profane
 Life's opportunities to gain,
And gather only worldly good ;
 But rather should my life fulfill
 The purpose of my Father's will,
  That over me it may be said,
  " Some struggling souls were helped and led,"
  When I am dead.

Life has no grander legacies
  For dying men to leave behind
  Than to be gratefully enshrined
In living hearts, by ministries
  Which recognize, and so embrace,
  The kin-ship of the human race :
    Far rather would I have it said
    That mine were such as this, instead,
      When I am dead.

DARNING STOCKINGS.

Last night, in my dreaming, I saw the dear face
Of Grandmother, sitting again in her place,
And weaving the thrums of her bright-colored yarn
In the rents of our stockings which she loved so to darn;
And I watched, as I used to, her smiles, as they
    played
In ripples of sunshine and blendings of shade,
While her fingers kept weaving the red and the blue,
With the skill of an artist, in rents that were new.

And back from the past came the trooping of feet
That fitted these stockings and socks so complete :
The mirth of their laughter again I could hear ;
The sobs of their crying came soft to my ear ;
The noise of their rollicking shouts, at their play,
And the bowing of heads as they all knelt to pray :
Like a sweet panorama it seemed to unroll,
And bind with its spell both my body and soul.

I saw her again, when the needle and yarn
Afforded no longer a pleasure to darn ;
When the sight of these stockings her tears would
      unlock,
For missing ones gone from her dear little flock ;
Some, out of the home to the mansions of rest,
And some to the welcoming plains of the West ;
And the stockings and yarn she had folded away,
Where her sweetest and tenderest memories lay.

Ah, memory ! how, with its beautiful sheen,
It floats up before us to keep our lives green,
And often its curtains so deftly unfold,
To keep our hearts young while our bodies grow old.
The circle no longer embraces them all,
Save up in that kingdom where no shadows fall ;
And all that is left are these memories fair
Of Grandmother's darning—except her old chair.

A FRAGMENT.

If Christ is half what He pretends to be,
    Then the admission is itself a call
    Commanding the attention of us all
To heed the voice of His authority.

And if acknowledged, then they toy with fate
    Who have the hardihood to disobey,
    Or linger at the threshold of the way,
With every moment that they hesitate.

IF WE KNEW.

Ah ! if humanity but knew
What mighty things a prayer might do
To still the tempest in the breast,
And bring the troubled spirit rest,
Their lips would not be half so slow
To frame the messages which go
Straight into that Almighty ear
Which bends so low these cries to hear.

If human thought were not so blind
To what the Father has designed,
It would not misinterpret so
The countless things we partly know,
And sometimes mis-apply the thought
Of plainest lessons which are taught,
Or turn to bitterness of gall
The grandest purposes of all.

If human hands could lift the veil,
And see how fervent prayers prevail
With Him whose promises they plead,
To teach humanity its need,
What inspiration would be lent
To plead for the impenitent,
And with what courage souls would dare
Beseige the throne of grace in prayer.

Ah ! if we only knew how near
And how acute the Father's ear
To catch the faintest breath of prayer,
Breathed upward any time or where,
And His facilities to send,
Even to earth's remotest end,
We'd see in this the swiftest way
To reach the souls for which we pray.

If we could come to see and feel
That every promise bears the seal
Of His eternal government,
As proof to us of their intent,
Would not the simplest common sense
Proclaim it as a grave offense
If we shall discount, from its face,
His promise at His throne of grace?

If only those who pray but knew
What mighty things a prayer may do,
They'd see that men upon their knees
Were stronger than Archimides.
And with such power underneath,
Would lift their fellows up from death,
And make th' eternal arches ring
With anthems which the ransomed sing.

"OF COURSE."

Two would-be suicides a week,
    And from the same prolific source,
Yet no one manifests surprise
    At what has simply come "of course."
"Of course" the victim must be jailed,
    That we may vindicate the laws,
But not, "of course," will be assailed
    The traffic which has been the cause.

"Of course" the tide of death flows on,
    As undisputed in its sway
As though its currents never bore
    A wife's or mother's hopes away.
"Of course" the people will regret
    The awful havoc which it makes,
And breathe some strong anathemas
    Against the courses which it takes.

"Of course" 'twill be some other name
    That forms the paragrapher's text,
When he informs us, as he will,
    Among his items, who is next ;
But on, and on, and on it runs,
    Year follows year, and still it pours
Its tide of death through trenches dug
    By our own hands, through all our doors.

"Of course" we may "restrain" its flow,
  And we may "regulate" its course ;
But can we stop its tide of woe
  Until we stop it at its source ?
"Of course" that never can be done
  Within a nationality
Where serfs and shackles are unknown,
  And every citizen is free !

"Of course," if men were sheep or swine,
  Our statesmen could devise a way
By which its sources should be reached,
  And rob it of its power to slay ;
But nothing is so cheap is men,
  And has as little worth as souls ;
And so we simply heave a sigh,
  While onward the death current rolls.

THE NEW GOSPEL.

How long would it take for the gospel of peace
  To spread through the earth and accomplish its
    mission
Of causing its meanness and sinning to cease,
  If now, at the last, we shall change its condition?
Instead of their thundering, " Thus saith the Lord,"
  Which prophets and preachers are always proclaim-
    ing,
Let sin be restricted by paying reward,
  Then wait for the devil to do the reclaiming.

How high must the price of the privilege be
    To prove a successful reformative measure,
Till lust shall be prisoned, from mountain to sea,
    However it clamor for profit or pleasure?
And what would give nerve to the arm of the law,
    Or strength to the hearts of the men who enforce
        them,
If those who transgress their enactments but saw
    That bribes to the conscience would quickly divorce
        them?

Has not the Great Teacher lacked wisdom to plan,
    In starting His scheme for the sinner's salvation,
Not knowing the needs or the weakness of man,
    Or methods most likely to his reformation?
What pity that wisdom so vital has lain
    These centuries long, by a cruel fate hidden,
Till brought to the light by a party campaign,
    To give to the nation its blessings unbidden!

How long will it take, at the marvellous rate
    At which the new gospel of truth is progressing,
Till hamlet and city and county and state
    Are happy and prosperous under its blessing?
What more can the "crankiest crank" still advise,
    To hasten the day of the nation's transforming,
Than here, in this gospel of high license lies,
    Which waits for a "license" to do the reforming?

And where will the logic of this gospel lead,
  And into what field may it not be extended?
And where is the meanness or villainous deed
  Which, under its teaching, may not be defended?
Then why should the hearts of the people be sad
  To witness the wretchedness stalking around them,
When, under these teachings, whatever is bad
  Is taxed to unburden the good that surrounds them?

What hinders the march of this truth, 'til it stands,
  Not only the dominant thought of this nation,
But sheds its beneficence over all lands,
  Until it has proven the power of salvation?
If only the hands of the "faithful" are joined—
  The old gospel christians to do all the praying—
While under the new, where the money is coined,
  The crooks and the villains shall do all the paying.

GROW BONE.

It's a mighty good thing to have muscle,
  In a world where there's so much to do,
Where the life is a tug and a tussle
  With the things it must build or subdue;
But the grip which keeps all the world spinning
  Is not muscle and sinew alone;
Every ounce of the power to do it
  Must depend on a lever of bone.

And if true in the lower creation,
  That all physical strength must depend
Quite as little on muscle contraction
  As on levers which never can bend,
Who will say it's not true in the higher,
  Where invisible forces control,
That a lever of bone is not needed
  To give power and grip to the soul ?

What a spectacle nature would give us,
  If, in order to make something stout,
She should fashion a muscular booby
  With the bones, for the levers, left out ?
Yet in morals there's no end of boobies
  Where the character hasn't a bone :
It can stand up as long as you hold it,
  But it never can stand up alone.

Yet it's worse than a slander to nature
  To say that she's fashioned a lout,
When the truth is so plain that the fibre
  Of strength to the soul is starved out.
If the future shall give us such heroes
  As the past of our nation has known,
Then the boys and the men of the present
  Need to diet, somewhat, to grow bone.

ONCE MORE.

This afternoon a raid was made on the houses of ill fame, and the station house was filled with the soiled doves that live in the various cotes of the city. Thirteen of them were arrested, the fines footing up to $425. The girls paid their fines and walked out to their homes to recoup the feathers of which they had been despoiled.—*Evening Tribune, June 25th, 1895.*

Once more the law is honored, which the sterner sex
      has made,
To squeeze out these "assessments" which these
      prostitutes have paid ;
This sex without a ballot, and with not a word to say
About the grade of their offence, or penalties they pay.
Like sheep before the shearer, when the law says
      "come," they come,
To let the shearers fleece them at their pleasure, and
      are dumb ;
And then return to pasture, and be happy that they
      may,
Because the ones who fleeced them might have sent
      them all away.

But will somebody tell us how this money which was
      paid
Is different from license fees for drivin' on their trade ?
It doesn't change the meanin' by the words with
      which we play,
Nor is it honest efforts for the puttin' crime away.

To say that they were "raided" or "arrested" might
    be true,
But not as those would understand who don't know
    how we do :
A notice from the Mayor or the Chief is all they need
To visit the Recorder, and instruct them how to plead.

And little time is wasted, for the thing is quickly done ;
The "fines" are gravely stated, and are settled, one
    by one ;
When every mother's daughter of them walks abroad
    as free
To prosecute their "calling" as a citizen can be.
And then we hug the phantom, and perhaps believe
    it true,
That this is all that justice and morality could do,
And give an inward chuckle at the business tact dis-
    played,
Which makes the city richer by the monies these have
    paid.

Oh, Justice ! is thy mission here so misinterpreted,
Or mammon has unseated thee, and reigneth in thy
    stead ?
Or we become so lecherous that lust is left to reign,
Like any other husbandry, for purposes of gain ?
And virtue left to languish and become an easy prey,
While vices riot everywhere for revenue they pay ?
If harlots made the laws themselves, or sat in Jus-
    tice's seat,
Could they do more than now is done, its purpose to
    defeat ?

WHO PAYS?

Corning's board of excise gathered in last year
$4,950, while Hornellsville's board received $4,415.
—*Daily papers.*

We thought that we were quite a town, accordin' to
    our size,
But Corning seems to beat us in her drinkin' enter-
    prise.
We don't know what to lay it to, the people or the
    glass,
Or to a higher license fee, that it has come to pass ;
But she is 'way ahead of us, the best that we can do,
By good five hundred dollars, in her whisky revenue ;
And we had ninety licenses, the excise board declare,
·Which made the city richer by contributin' their share.

And that's a license granted, as most any one can see,
For just a fraction over each one hundred thirty-three
Of our twelve thousand people, and they all of them
    survive,
And many are reputed to not only live but thrive.
Now, figure up their livin' and their license fees and
    rent,
And money which they pay for "stock," and it's a
    nice per cent,
Without the profits laid aside for rainy days, or age,
From such a little colony as forms their patronage.

There must be quite a margin in the "merchandise"
      they sell,
To have so small a patronage support them all so well,
For of the hundred thirty-three, as average would fall,
Another large per cent of these don't buy their
      "goods" at all.
Take out a half for women—most of whom, we love
      to think,
Have too much sterling common sense to buy such
      stuff to drink ;
And then subtract the boys and girls who either are
      too small
Or have been too well trained to drink, and where'll
      the average fall ?

Then take the fifth, or sixth, or tenth, or what per
      cent it be,
Whom they can call their customers, and any one can
      see
That if they had to pay it in the form of common tax,
It would not only make them "kick," but almost
      break their backs.
A little fifteen cents a day, which many spend for
      beer,
Will grow to fifty dollars if they keep it up a year ;
And fifty dollars laide aside, or loaned at some per
      cent,
Would soon provide a little home, where now they
      have to rent.

But where's the sense of talkin' facts to those who
 love to drink,
For it would not be needed if they'd ever stop to
 think?
The logic of a ground-hog would convince him mighty
 soon
That burrows were as good for him as for the skunk
 or coon;
And not unless compelled to by the rigid force of law
Would he be fool enough to dig their burrows with
 his paw:
But men, who might think if they would, will not
 alone provide
For other households than their own, but kill themselves beside.

And where's the sense of askin' them who pays the
 license fees,
When they are satisfied to work while landlords take
 their ease,
And then as soon as pay day comes will make their
 wages fly
In payin' up the weekly score, or treatin' company?
Who pays? We think the drinkers' wives contribute
 quite a share,
By goin' without things they need, and eatin' scanty
 fare;
His children, too, contribute, by the rags they wear
 to school,
Or stayin' out and growin' up a vagabond or fool.

What wisdom in a policy, for city or a state,
To foster institutions which directly militate
Against the manhood of its men, or sanctity of home,
Or breeds a moral pestilence for those who are to come?
Who pays?   The state and nation, in the citizen
    made clown,
Or shut behind some prison bars, his manhood broken
    down,
Who, but for such a policy, which swallows men as
    prey,
Would never have adventured into such a downward
    way.

Who pays?   Let's stop and ask it, let us ask it o'er
    and o'er,
Till something like the naked truth shall dawn on us
    once more,
And we shall see this revenue with such awakened
    sense
That we can clearly comprehend just what it repre-
    sents.
Let's ask it till a clearer light enables us to see
That nations cannot long survive on taxed iniquity,
But that by God's eternal law, though recognized or
    not,
Iniquity for revenue will generate a rot.

We won't dispute with Corning in the eminence at-
    tained,
Nor feel humiliated by advantage she has gained,

In filchin', indirectly, from the pockets of her poor
So large a sum of money, for enough lies at our door.
Our ninety licensed places, which are open night and
  day,
Have proven all sufficient to absorb the poor man's
  pay ;
And we have shown our meanness by the way we
  work our street
With money which his family needs, and make him a
  dead-beat.

FOLDED HANDS.

The world is full of prophets who are able to foresee
The perils which confront us, and to tell what ought
  to be ;
They sit at every cross-road, and in every country
  store,
And stand in knots upon our streets, or go from door
  to door,
And tell how churches should be run to keep them
  from a rut,
And what destroys our commerce, causing factories to
  shut ;
And tell, with much precision, what such times as
  these demand,
While nineteen out of twenty rarely think to lend a
  hand.

Say, brother, if you see it, why not lend your little
    mite
To make the wrong conditions you complain of nearer
    right?
Instead of growing eloquent about what should be
    done,
Work out an object lesson in at least the life of one;
Show what a pretty jewel some consistency may be,
Worked into every-day affairs, where common folks
    can see;
And make your life as helpful as you think the times
    demand,
By using what facilities you have at your command.

If churches are not running as it seems to you they
    should,
To be in your community the greatest power for good,
There ought to be suggested to a person who is wise
A remedy that's better than to simply criticize.
And so about the evils of the city or the state,
They're never any greater than the citizens create;
And they who want things better cannot issue their
    commands,
With any great consistency, and sit with folded hands.

If you have any grievance with the church or with
    the state,
Do something more to help it than to simply execrate;
Your individuality should count for something more
Than words of execration for the things which you
    deplore.

It doesn't take a hero or a prophet to behold
Some things in either church or state about which
    they can scold :
It does require some courage of the better sort to stand
For every form of righteousness, and lend a helping
    hand.

It seems a little curious that any forms of vice
Could meet with public favor, for a stipulated price,
And gain the state's protection to a system which
    controls
The action and the conscience of the people at the
    polls ;
But no one need denounce it and complain of what
    they see,
In all its carnival of crimes, and its debauchery,
Until they cease their yielding to its clamorous de-
    mands,
And offer more resistance than to sit with folded
    hands.

And, brother, if some things occur you cannot quite
    approve,
Or even fill with your distress, within the church you
    love,
Would the Redeemer's kingdom be advanced in any
    wise
If you should hold yourself aloof, and simply criti-
    cise ?

To clearly see an evil may be half a victory,
But courage will be needed to apply the remedy.
If wrongs creep into church or state, their presence
 there demands
That they should be ejected by some active, vigorous
 hands.

THE SINGER AND THE SONG.

It was not the voice of a seraph which stole,
In cadence of song, through my ears to my soul,
This bright Sabbath morning, with message so sweet
The ages can only the story repeat ;
But a voice wholly human (a voice, still, so dear
That one may be pardoned for loving to hear),
And the song and the voice were uniting to say
That "Jesus is tenderly calling to-day."

Ah ! "tenderly calling" but faintly express
His infinite longing to help and to bless ;
To stretch out His arm and deliver to-day,
If only our answer shall tell Him He may.
Then softly there came from the singer again,
In the line of my thoughts, such a plaintive refrain,
That "some one shall knock, when the doors shall be
 shut,"
And hear a voice answering "I know you not."

And I pictured a soul at the beautiful gate,
Desiring to enter, and found it too late ;
And fancied I stood where I plainly could see
What a sad disappointment such answer must be.
The singer went on, with my thoughts keeping pace,
Through the mazes of music and marvels of grace,
To "almost persuaded is only to fail,"
And "doom comes at last with its sad, bitter wail."

These songs and these thoughts sent a wonderful
        thrill
Of joy to my heart and of strength to my will,
That, "tenderly calling" to me, I would say,
Yes, gracious Redeemer, come even to-day,
And make of my life what Thy wisdom shall see
Is most for Thy glory and better for me,
That when I shall come to the beautiful gate,
A "welcome" shall greet me, instead of "too late."